# The Mind Hunter

## Elisa Kensington

# CONTENTS

# CHAPTER 1

Today is the day. I start my first day at my new job. Moving to London has been a big change, and while yes, I will miss my job in my hometown, I am sure adventures await with this one. Excited to start my new day, I run to my closet, throw on a blue dress and some black heels, and throw my raven hair into a bun before heading out to go to work.

After a 10-minute drive, I arrive at Oak Valley Psychiatric Hospital to start my day. Walking in, I can't help but notice how gloomy all the nurses look. Everyone looks dreadful! Yes, we may all work with those who are insane, however, we can't become insane ourselves. We need to smile. I dismiss my gloomy co-workers and head to the office to greet the head doctor.

I knock on his door and he yells for me to come in. He seems....lovely. I open the door, make my way to his desk, and sit down across from him. I smile politely.

"Hello, sir," I say with a soft smile on my face.

He glances at me for a minute and returns to his computer typing away. "You're the new one?" He looked me up and down with no expression on his face. "Here is your first patient." He says while tossing me a quite thick folder. "Nurse Amelia will take you to your office." He gestures to the Nurse to walk me out.

I thank him and follow the nurse to my office. After she leaves, I take a glance through the folder. How exciting! While I read over the folder, a couple of things immediately jumped out at me. He is known for murdering his past shrinks. How lucky I am. It was unsettling, but exciting to be dealing with someone different. I looked at my watch and noticed that I have 30 minutes until my first session with him.

There is not much about his childhood, no siblings, no family, and no friends. How sad. I study his folder some more before preparing myself for the session. I walk down the halls and approach the last door on the left. I tighten my grip on my notebook and take a deep breath before walking into the interrogation room. I noticed he was strapped to his chair, it almost pained my heart to see this.

He fixed his cold glare on me and smirked, "Come to fix me?"

I remove my coat and sit across from him. "No," I stated bluntly.

"Then what are you doing here?" His words came out sharp and sarcastic, he kept the same glaring look.

I leaned on the table a bit and stared directly into his piercing baby-blue eyes. "To learn you."

"And what do you plan on doing with that information?" His body stayed completely stiff, he didn't move his head even an inch, but I swore it felt like he was staring straight through me.

I lean back in my chair to seem relaxed. "I'm not sure yet, maybe I will figure it out as we go along," I say with a slight smile.

"Figure me out?" His gaze didn't change in the slightest, but it felt like he was analyzing me. "You do realize I have killed 23 people, 23 people who were just trying to 'fix' me" He scoffed at the last bit, he seemed to find it incredibly amusing that people thought they could figure him out and change him.

"Who said I was here to fix you?" I asked.

"Hm." He thought for a moment, his mind seemingly working overtime. "A fair point." There was nothing more I could do or say to push his buttons, he seemed calm. His look never changed but something deeper was going on behind it. "Are you looking for my weaknesses, then? Are you here out of pure interest?" He shrugged, he was genuinely curious.

I pull out my notebook and write down some notes. "I am here to learn about you, so I would assume need to know both strengths and weaknesses."

"I wish the other 23 knew that." A flash of anger crossed through his features, but it was quickly suppressed. He watched me write in my notebook. "What are you writing?" He smirked.

"You want to know what I am writing?" I asked while smiling

"Well, I am a bit curious." A small smile crept on his face, he seemed relaxed in his seat, chained to the chair and yet he still exuded a sense of danger.

"My first impression of you," I state while closing the notebook.

"And what is that? Don't be afraid to offend me." He said with a smug grin waiting for my response.

"Arrogant, but sad. You are truly a sad case." I said bluntly hoping to get some reaction out of him.

The comment seemed to catch him off guard. He smirked as he looked away for a moment. My comment seemed to affect him. "And why do you suppose I'm sad? What could you possibly know about me?"

"I can see you are a coward." I grabbed my notes and continued writing my thoughts.

"A coward?" The words left an ugly impression on his face and his eyes widened. They widened because I had hit a nerve, and he took offense to the word. "I am many things," He said, his tone sharp, "But I'm no coward."

"You killed 23 people because they wanted to get to know you and possibly fix you. You killed them because you were scared they could fix you and what they might find about you." I stared directly into his eyes waiting for his reaction.

"I did what I had to." The words were sharp, his tone was sharp. He looked directly at me, but I could see that he was struggling to not show any emotion even though he was clearly getting riled up about the subject. "I don't need to be fixed. All of those people tried to fix me, tried to change me, but I am perfectly fine the way I am."

"I agree."

"You agree?" His tone was sarcastic, and the corners of his lips turned into a smile. "So I don't need to be fixed."

"I feel like you need to be understood."

Those words caught him off guard again, once again he looked away from me. Something was going on inside him, he was analyzing his thoughts, maybe even starting to rethink them to some degree, But even though he would never admit it, he seemed interested in me. "And you would be the one to understand....me?"

I pondered a minute on his question and answered honestly. "I am not sure, but I would like to try."

Those words felt like music to his ears. His gaze slowly turned back to me, and he stayed silent for a moment before speaking. "The world would be a better place if you had been my psychiatrist first."

I smiled warmly at him. "I will see you tomorrow morning Archer."

"I am going to start looking forward to it." He smirked leaning back in his seat. When I left, I could feel him watching me as I left.

The first day was done, and it wasn't as bad as I assumed, I didn't die, so that's a plus.

# CHAPTER 2

It was the next day and I couldn't be more ready to start my day. I went to my closet and picked out a white button-up shirt and a black skirt. I made breakfast and took some to-go, I figured I would share some with Archer. I hopped in my car to head to work. I walked into my office to see my boss in there waiting for me.

"I'm impressed. Most shrinks are dead within the first hour," he stated nonchalantly.

"You are a man with many words, how kind." I blurted back. His attitude towards me was really annoying.

He snorted, unamused. "Just be careful Ms.Jones."

I take a quick glance through Archer's file again to see what we should talk about today. I have gathered a few topics in mind and with that, I leave and head to the interrogation room. Seeing him in those binds hurt my heart again. I know he was deemed legally insane, but it still hurt. I sat down and laid the breakfast out for him to eat and asked the guards to unbind his hands but keep his feet strapped down.

The guards unchained him from the table but kept his feet tethered together like I said. As Archer sat down and started eating I noticed he seemed less angry, less cold, maybe even a little less dangerous than before. I felt in control of him.

"Do you like it?" I asked, in hopes he would.

"Yes, it's quite good." He nodded his head, even his smile was a bit less sharp. I noticed with every bite of food he took, he seemed to become less tense and more like himself. When he finished his last bite, he looked up at me.

"I have a few topics I would like to discuss today with you."

"Sure, what's on your mind?" He had finished eating the food, and the smile was still on his face, a bit less sharp than before. It was clear he was starting to like me, in a nonromantic sense. But he also liked me..in a different way.

"The patient Elizabeth. You had broken out of your room multiple times and started a relationship with her. Can you tell me more about that?" I asked while grabbing my notebook.

The smile disappeared from his face entirely, he went back to being serious. His face darkened, and he looked down at the table as if he was deep in thought. He was thinking about the Elizabeth situation, whether he wanted to revisit that thought or avoid it completely, whether he wanted to tell me about it or keep it a secret. After a moment he spoke. "She was probably the only one who ever treated me..with respect."

I write this down in my notes. "How did she treat you with respect?"

"She never tried to change me or fix me, she didn't care that I was labeled as insane, she didn't care that I was dangerous even." He thought about it for another moment. "She didn't really care about anything except getting to know *me*, the person behind the label. She liked *me*, not this fake 'fixable' person that everyone else wanted me to pretend to be."

I pause at his statement. How sweet he has felt this before. "Has anyone else ever shown this type of affection to you?"

"No." The words were sharp and short. Elizabeth was probably the first one he'd ever let get through to him like that. He continued eating and thought for a minute before his face darkened again. "She's dead." Those words were said with a bit of sadness. "I guess I was too attached to her, too dependent. I lost my temper, lost control, and I killed her. After that event, I decided to never let myself get attached to anyone again."

I stiffened a bit at his remark, but I am a professional so I can't allow it to get to me. "Tell me, what caused you to get angry?"

There was a slight pause, his face darkened again, a small twitch of his hand. "I caught her betraying me." The words were sharp, and there was no emotion in them whatsoever. He didn't seem to care about Elizabeth or her betrayal of him, he didn't even seem to care that he killed her. He'd probably do it again if he could. "My temper is what caused me to react the way I did."

I write down in my notes everything he has said so far. "Can you go into detail about the betrayal?"

"She was talking about me, sharing my secrets, things that were told between her and I." He seemed slightly angered just by the thought of it. "I couldn't help but get mad, and when I got mad.." He didn't finish the sentence, his tone was sharp, and his eyes were hard to look at.

I sat my notebook down. "This is a safe place. Continue. What did you do?" I said with a comforting voice.

His hand twitched again, and he seemed to get lost in thought again. "I lost control. I lost my temper. I killed her, and the people that were trying to protect her." His voice had become more monotone and less sharp. "I remember my thoughts after the fact, I knew exactly what I had done. I didn't feel regret, I didn't feel a damn thing."

I nod my head. "Thank you for sharing."

"Can I ask you something?" His voice was still flat, completely monotone, but there was a slight hint that he wanted to know something.

"Of course."

He thought for a minute, as if he was trying to find the words to express himself properly. "How do you think I see you?" The question was completely genuine.

I pondered for a moment on the question. Elizabeth and I seemed to share things in common. "I would say you see me as Elizabeth and you are scared of that."

That seemed to catch him off guard and he was visibly surprised that I had guessed that right away. The surprise was only there for a moment before he hid his face with a blank stare and emotionless tone. He'd gotten comfortable with me, he had even started to trust me to some degree, and now I have made him realize how much I resemble Elizabeth. And in his mind, I was likely going to betray him like she did once I found out what he really was.

"I knew what I was getting myself into when I became your shrink. Your secrets are safe with me." I winked.

He stared at me as if he was really analyzing me, trying to see if he could trust me like he trusted Elizabeth. There was silence for a moment before he spoke. "That's exactly what Elizabeth said."

"I don't expect you to believe, I am aware actions speak louder than words."

"I guess they do." His tone was cold, but he was thinking. He thought for a moment, his eyes still boring into mine while he analyzed everything about me. "Does that mean if I tell you something, you'll keep it to yourself?"

"Would it make you feel better if I told you one of my secrets first?" I asked hoping to gain some trust.

He paused for a moment before speaking."Sure, that seems fair." He seemed to be analyzing the whole idea behind that, it seemed like something that had never been offered to him before.

"I will tell you my secret during our next session. Sadly, our hour is up for the day." I grab my belongings and allow the doctors to bind his hands back down.

"Ok." He stayed silent for a moment before speaking."Can I ask you a question before you go?"

"Of course," I said, as I tilted my head.

"Do you know if the doctors are monitoring our conversations in here?" He looked out the room a bit but he was still facing me. He seemed to think there was a possibility the doctors were keeping a close eye on him, but he also seemed to doubt in his mind that they were doing that.

"Yes. If you would like, we can have our session in my office tomorrow so you can feel more comfortable speaking freely." I suggested.

"I'd like that." He nodded his head."But do you know how much the doctors are listening to? Do they hear everything we are saying?" As much as he was interested in having privacy, he was also intrigued by how private they'd actually allow this session to be.

"In the interrogation room, everything is recorded. We are on camera, in my office, there are no cameras, no recordings."

"I see." The thought of possibly being recorded didn't sit well with him, he didn't feel as though he was able to be 100% genuine, because he didn't know how many ears were listening in. But hearing that none of the conversations in my office were being recorded really intrigued him. And he did trust me more here than he did anyone else in the entire place, even if the trust was only a smidge.

"It's settled. I will see you in my office tomorrow."

"Alright, I'll be looking forward to it." He seemed genuinely interested in seeing how the sessions would go. "I hope you know that by allowing me to speak freely to you, you've made yourself my target." His smile was sharp. "I will always do my best to remain honest with you, but you will also be the one person I'll be looking to use and manipulate."

"I will be looking forward to it." With that, I leave and head to the head doctor's office.

# CHAPTER 3

The head doctor was in his office, typing something into the computer and he looked up as I entered. "I noticed you are taking an interest in our most interesting patient, so I was wondering if I could have a word with you."

"Of course, sir."

"How would you rate your first session with him?" The head doctor spoke without even looking up from his computer.

"Enlightening."

"He's an interesting one, isn't he?" The man spoke with his eyes averted, he was typing away at his computer still and his tone wasn't sharp or angry. "I trust you've been careful with what you've been saying to him?"

"I have. I do have one thing I would like to discuss with you." I stated before approaching his desk.

"Please, say what's on your mind." He looked up at me, seeming genuinely curious and perhaps even a bit concerned.

"I wondered if it would be okay if my patient and I could have our sessions in my office from now on?" I asked, hoping he wouldn't find me too insane.

The doctor looked off to the side and thought about it for a moment."I don't see why not, you've made good progress and you might be the only person who can genuinely connect with him properly." He thought about it a moment more. "Just make sure you know what you're doing and make sure he doesn't get attached to you like he did with Elizabeth."

I nod my head.

I started driving home from work and prepare myself for bed, nervous about what tomorrow brings. I fall away into a sweet slumber pretty quickly, today had worn me out.

I wake up to my alarm blaring in my ear, and jump up to get ready for the day. I get dressed, do my hair, and make breakfast fo the two of us again, then head to work. I arrive in my office to see Archer is already there, strapped to a chair.

His eyes are wide open, looking at me as I enter the room. Without even waiting for me to speak, he spoke."Good, you didn't lie about it being private in here." There was another pause as he waited for me to speak, he was looking dead into my eyes this entire time and I could tell he was analyzing every inch of my face.

I laid out breakfast and had him completely untied from his chair.

When he was untied, he instantly got up and grabbed some food, after eating what he wished, he spoke."So can I ask you a question?" His tone was a bit sharp, not completely like before but still sharp.

"Yes," I stated intrigued.

His gaze bore deep into mine and didn't move. He sat with his arms crossed, looking at me intensely."Why would a nice woman like you want to help someone as dangerous as me? How did you manage to build so much empathy?"

I stared back into his eyes before answering. "To be frank. it's my job. I didn't have a choice of my patients you were handed to me. I have grown empathy for you because it seems as though you were dealt with bad cards in life."

"What makes you think I was dealt bad cards in life?" He seemed intrigued by the statement but his face didn't show it. He had a stone-cold serious face but when I looked a bit deeper, I could see a lot of pain in his eyes.

"Your folder. There is no mention of family or friends. I assume you were a lonely child." I said in a sad tone.

His body froze and his breath caught in his chest, he seemed stunned by the accuracy of my statement. This was surprising to him.He stared at me quietly for a moment before he finally spoke."My parents died when I was twelve, it was just me in the world for a while." His tone was sharp as usual, but it had a tinge of sadness in it.

"How did your parents die?"

He seemed a bit caught off guard by the question, his breathing seemed to pick up as he thought about it. The sadness in his tone became a bit stronger and genuine. "I guess I never told anyone in this place. My mother died a long time ago, she went too deep into her work and ended up taking her own life." He paused for a second after that, he took a deep breath."My father couldn't deal with the pain, all the sorrow I was feeling when we both lost her broke him, and a few days later he followed her."

"I am sorry to hear that. Remember when I told you I would share one of my secrets with you?"

He sat up in his seat at the mention of secrets, he was very curious as to what kind of secret I would share with him. What could I have going on in my personal life that was dark enough to be considered a secret? "That's right, I almost forgot."

"My secret is, you and I are very much alike," I stated.

He stared at me as the meaning began to process in his head. "How are we alike?" He stared directly into my eyes as he waited for an answer, a small frown came across his face as he thought about the entire thing.

"Do you think we are alike?" I questioned.

"Are we?" He asked. The frown on his face grew even more as he wondered why I would even bring that up. "I really don't see anywhere where we are alike. I am.." He thought for a m oment."I'm a psychopath. I have no empathy, no feelings, and I'm an emotionally numb individual who can't feel anything."

"What if I told you I too have murdered someone?" I raise my eyebrow.

His entire body froze, and his eyes grew wide, and his jaw dropped partially."You have?" He sounded shocked by the news but it was hard to hide the admiration and excitement behind it, he was staring into my eyes with complete awe and he looked almost awestruck that I had that kind of secret to hide.

"Yes."

"How many?" He was practically beaming with admiration, I being so similar to him meant so much to him. He was so happy to see some kind of similar quality in someone.

"37." I stated.

His eyes grew even wider and he paused for a second, he didn't know what to say or what to feel about this news. "37?" He paused again, he didn't even know how he should process that information."Who were they?"

"My friends and family."

He paused once again, and finally, he just spoke his thoughts out loud."God damn." That was all he said because it was all he knew what to think about the whole thing.The information was new to him but he was already starting to feel a bit of a connection with me. I was completely different from anyone else he'd ever met.

"How does this make you feel?"

"It's a bit shocking, but I guess it makes me feel a little less alone." He had never known anyone who could have a history like that, no one who had killed so many people. "I feel a lot more comfortable around you now."

"Good!" I said confidently. I was happy we were able to make some sort of connection.

"Can I ask what the circumstances were for those murders?" He was curious about the details of the murders, he wanted to know if they were a spur-of-the-moment decision or if they were planned and calculated. For him, most of his killings just happened because he felt like it, his anger just got the better of him and he snapped. He'd never really planned any of them.

"There were reasons, yes. However, I will have to answer those in our next session. Our time is up for today." The doctors came in and tied him back down and escorted him out of the room.

"Alright, I'll look forward to it." He didn't really want the session to end but he would respect my request and wait patiently for the next session.

# Chapter 4

I walk into the Doctor's office to greet him, he had sent me a message last night asking me to come in and speak with him. The doctor was at his desk when I arrived, he seemed lost in thought. He heard the door open and he looked up and noticed I had entered the room, he didn't speak, and he just waited for me to speak.

"You wanted to see me, sir?"

"Yes, please take a seat." The doctor waited for me to sit down, his whole focus was on me.

I felt a bit intimated with his stare towards me, however, I couldn't help but notice that he was a handsome man.

The doctor noticed I was eyeing him, and he seemed to smile at it. Then he quickly switched back to a very emotionless demeanor, it was almost like he caught himself smiling and felt like he had to be professional. It was quite endeari ng."I have a question for you."

"Yes sir?"

"I feel as though something you're doing in that office is causing a connection between you and one of my more problematic patients, the one who goes by the name of Archer Williams. You're bringing out qualities in him that I've never seen before, and I wish to know what exactly you are doing to cause this."

I chuckled a bit. "If you a concerned about me catching feelings for him, you have no reason to be. I am simply just trying to find ways to connect with him so he can feel comfortable talking with me."

The doctor nodded his head. He thought about what I said and after a few seconds, he spoke."I see, it's good that you aren't taking any sort of liking to him, however, I want to make sure you understand that you are handling a very dangerous patient. Be careful how you deal with him, he is very manipulative and I believe he hasn't shown you his true character just yet."

I was shocked, he has never shown any genuine concern for me since I started working here. "Are you worried about me?"

The doctor froze for a second, he seemed surprised by my question and he stared at me with widened eyes. He wasn't quite sure how to respond to that, in this place, care is never shown towards the employees. But he had grown a bit of a soft spot for me. He didn't answer right away, he just stared at me for a moment before answering. "Yes."

I smiled. "How sweet."

There was a moment of silence after my statement before the doctor spoke again. "And I still would like you to be more careful around him, he is a manipulator and a murderer. If he catches you off guard, you could find yourself in a very bad situation."

"I understand." After my statement, I went to my office to see Archer sitting at my desk.

I didn't really expect him to be there yet, and when I walked in, I was taken aback with him here. He looked up at me and stared. "Are you just going to staring at me?" His tone was blunt but I had to admit it was quite entertaining, the two of us just making eye contact without saying anything was quite funny.

I raised my eyebrow. "And are you just going to keep sitting in my seat?"

"Yes." He spoke with the same bluntness as before. "It's very comfortable and it has a nice vantage point, your desk has the perfect angle of being able to see the door." He was looking away now but he still didn't get off the seat.

"I see. May I have my seat back?" I asked, politely.

"Why should I give you your seat back? It's much more comfortable here." His tone was blunt, but almost playful.

"I see." I sat in the seat across from him. "Very well then."

"So, I have a question." He said after a moment of silence.

"Yes?"

"What would happen if I refused to give your seat back? Would you just force me to get off?" He said with a somewhat childish smirk on his face, he was teasing me.

"I guess I would have to order the doctors to strap you to my seat since you like it so much," I said in a teasing tone back.

That gave him a bit of a chuckle. "And if they did would you just stand there and watch? Or would you try to pull me off? I would fight you if you tried." He continued to tease me.

"I would watch."

He had a playful and almost childish smirk on his face as he continued to speak in the same teasing tone. "Would it be entertaining to watch me get strapped down to your seat and then watch as you sit on top of me? Maybe that's why you want me to keep this seat so bad. So you can watch as I struggle?"

"Oh calm yourself, I would never sit on a patient." I laughed.

His smile became a bit wider then he spoke again. "No? Not even me? How come? I have the most perfect and most gorgeous face in this entire psychiatric facility." He was still kidding but I would swear his ego got the best of him sometimes.

"Because I am your psychiatrist, Not a playmate."

"So you see me as a patient, nothing more?" He said quite innocently. He was looking directly into my eyes with those piercing white eyes of his. "Is it wrong of me to get the feeling like you see me as more than a patient sometimes though?"

"No. However, we are not here to talk about how I view you. Tell me, where are you from Archer?" I asked, attempting to change the subject.

He seemed to grow a bit frustrated that I changed the subject and he seemed to get a bit pouty. "I was born in a small town not too far from here, and my family is from the same area. Is that all you'd like to know? Where are you from?"

"I am from Bristol."

"Bristol? That's quite far from here." He sat there for a moment before adding. "How'd you end up here so far away from home?"

"I needed a change in scenery," I said in a calming tone.

His expression grew a little more serious, suddenly I could feel something shift in his body language. It was like a flip switch on. "How were things back in Bristol?"

"Boring. Why the sudden shift in your body?"

He paused for a moment before he spoke, it was like he was holding his breath but he didn't say anything. The shift in his body was quite dramatic, his tone became extremely serious and his facial features were now almost completely blank. The only thing he spoke was a single word. "Boring?"

"Yes. Boring."

His whole body was like a statue now, his face was emotionless and blank. The only difference was the way he was staring at me. It was like he was looking right through me. The whole environment seemed to change, it was almost as if his mere presence was causing the whole room to turn somber. His eyes almost looked as if they were staring through a mirror into my own soul. He spoke again, but it was so much more serious than anything he'd ever spoken before, he was completely monotone and his tone was very harsh. "Boring?"

"Yes. How many times are we going to repeat this same word?"

"I want you to elaborate." He said in the same harsh tone. His body was still like a statue, but the whole room felt heavy. It was almost as if he was making sure I knew that I didn't make him laugh or smile ever again like I did before. As he got more serious the whole room seemed to turn a darker shade, like when the sun went down. He stared me down and I could almost see the anger and sadness in his eyes.

"And I wanted to know why your body shifted, but you did not answer that. So why should I provide you an answer?"

"The simple answer is that you made me angry." He said rather softly. There was no anger in his voice or face, he said it with coldness and seriousness. "I was fine when we were joking around earlier but that 'boredom' of yours struck a chord in me. Are you just going to keep dismissing my questions?"

"I am your shrink, it's my job to ask questions and get to know you. If you don't like it, you could always ask for a different shrink." I stated, coldly.

"Is that what you think? That I dislike talking to you? That's not true." His tone became sharper, I could sense his rage building inside of him. "I don't dislike talking to you, I dislike *what* we're talking about. It reminds me of horrible memories that I choose to avoid thinking about. I was having a fun time just minutes ago, what caused this sudden change?"

"So me asking you where you were from, brought up memories?"

He paused for a moment and I could feel the tension in the air. Then he finally spoke."Yes. They did, very horrible memories."

"Tell me about them."

"Do you really want to hear about them?" He asked me, his tone shifting again. He said it in quite a different and kinder tone than before.

"Yes."

He sighed and sat back in his seat. "You have to promise me one thing before I tell you though. You can't tell a single soul whatever I'm going to say to you."

"I promise."

He then sat there for a moment as if he was gathering his thoughts. When he finally spoke his tone was blunt but he spoke at a much faster pace."Okay. I grew up in a not-so-well-off neighborhood, my home life was never the best. I never had the best relationship with my parents and my siblings. My mom was emotionally abusive to me and my siblings and my dad was never home very much. When they did argue I had to try and break it up which was probably a bad decision because my parents always took that out on me later."

"What happened to your siblings after your parents died?"

"They went down different paths...They all had their own problems from growing up in that household. They each dealt with their traumas in different ways. My older brother became a heavy drug addict, my younger sister became very mentally unstable. To be frank everyone in my family was messed up in their own individual way."

"Unique."

"Yes, in their own ways, each of them was quite unique when it came to their trauma. Each of them was a mess in their own way."

"You speak of them in past tense, are they dead?"

"No." He spoke with a flat voice when he answered. "They're still alive, I just don't talk or associate with them much anymore. I try and keep my distance, they all remind me of what I went through. They all trigger me, so it's best if I keep my distance."

"I see." I start to write down my notes.

Archer watched me for a moment before he asked me a question. "Do you write down *everything* I tell you? It feels like you're writing a book about me."

"I write down what stands out to me," I explained.

"So what is it that stood out about that? The fact that I grew up in a dysfunctional family? The fact that I suffered from abuse? What is it that made you write it down?"

"Yes. it definitely contributes to the person who you are today."

"So you think I'm a mess then?" He said with slight irritation in his tone. I could tell he didn't like getting called out, although I had to admit that he was right. I was writing down exactly what he was saying and it was most likely going to be used to make a psychological profile of him.

"Did I say you were a mess?"

"No, you didn't say those exact words, but you made it pretty obvious."

"Do you remember what I told you on the first day?"

"What exactly are you referring to? You've said quite a bit."

I laughed. "I told you I didn't want to fix you, but to try and understand you. That is why I write down what stands out to me."

"So basically you're saying that I have a lot of problems then?" He was trying to be a little more playful with this comment but I could tell it had an underlining of anger underneath it.

"You are in a psych ward for murdering, of course, you have a lot of problems." I laughed. "However, no that is not what I am saying."

"Then care to explain what you mean?" He said in an almost mocking tone, I could tell his patience and ego were taking a hit from my answers.

"You love to argue don't you?"

"I do." He said immediately with no hesitation. He had a slight smirk on his face and while it was hard to tell with his tone of voice and his cold blank expression, I could tell he was enjoying this.

"I hope you have enjoyed your fun, however, our time is now up, I will see you tomorrow," I stated with a smirk. I have the doctors come in remove him from my seat and strap him back to his.

He sat there silently, he had never felt like such an idiot. He had been outplayed in every aspect of this conversation. He was trying not to show how much his ego was being bruised and his anger was rising. He let out a sigh and let the doctors take him away. He'd come up with a plan to really make me see his bad side tomorrow, it was the only way he could save his ego now.

# CHAPTER 5

As I was getting ready for the morning, I wondered how long he had been staying in the facility. I was also thinking about my plans for the weekend. I made my way to my office and once again, my boss had texted me to come in and speak to him.

My boss, Jonathan, seemed to be on his phone and looked up when he noticed I was already there. He then gestured for me to come into his office and sit across from him. I sat across from him and waited for him to speak, I was unsure why he wanted to see me.

After a moment of silence, he looked up from his phone. "So, how did the session with Archer go yesterday?"

"A little disheartening, I seemed to upset him yesterday. However, I am confident today will be better."

He chuckled a bit. "You always say that, yet it seems like that man is always upset with you. Maybe you should reconsider your approach, don't you think? You haven't made much progress with him."

I wondered what he meant by that. I mean, I have lasted longer than his past shrinks so surely that counts for something. "May I ask what you mean? I feel like my progress may be slow, for sure, but I still am making some."

He sighed, it seemed like I was not just not getting it. "Do you really not realize why he's always upset with you? I thought you were a psychologist. It was almost like you did that on purpose to make him upset. I don't care if you think it's for his own good, how about you actually try and help him instead of making him even more unstable? That doesn't seem like a very good approach to your job, does it?"

Anger arose in me, but I took a breath and stared at my boss. "I have to get to know him in order to help him, and sometimes that means I need to ask the most difficult of questions," I said while plastering the fakest smile I could.

Jonathan scoffed and was silent for a moment before he spoke once again. "That's the thing, you keep asking really difficult questions that only get him more angry. You keep striking nerves that seem like they're incredibly sensitive for him. Is it really that bad for me to ask you to change your approach to actually help him? How long till you have your next appointment with him?"

I sighed, knowing that this conversation was not going anywhere. "Forgive me, for I am on edge today. I was not trying to argue. My next session is in 30 minutes."

He sighed as well, it seemed this conversation was going nowhere. He didn't even want to keep arguing with me. "That is quite alright. So, what do you plan on doing with him today? More questions that will just upset him more?"

At that moment, it took everything in me not to, what do the Americans call it? Yes, lose my shit. I cleared my throat and answered his question. "I will focus on light-hearted topics for today is Friday, the happiest of all weekdays."

He laughed at that last part a little bit and he nodded his head. "Good, I'm happy to hear that. Just please, avoid any topics that will get Archer mad. The longer you keep him calm the more likely you'll be able to get to the truth underneath his problems. If you can't, then we'll have to find a more suitable psychologist for him. And I doubt *anyone* would be willing to take on that challenge."

I nod my head, walk out of the office, and head into mine, where I see Archer waiting for me.

Like always, he was strapped to his chair and he was just glaring at the door, waiting for me to come through. As I entered my office he didn't say a word or make a sound yet his glare was like razor-sharp and piercing through me. I could sense the anger in his eyes.

I sat down across from him sighing. "It's Friday, why are we angry today?"

His glare never once broke, he had a look of such rage in his eyes that it was almost like he was ready for the moment when I had asked him the wrong question so he could blow. He was trying to restrain himself but I could tell that at the slightest wrong comment he'd let it all out. He didn't speak a word.

I arched an eyebrow "Are we ignoring me today?"

He finally spoke, but the sound of his voice was rather hushed and almost like he was muttering under his breath. "I don't feel like talking today. I'm not in the mood to be asking or answering any of your stupid questions."

"Ah is that how it is today? I will be gone the next two days so you won't be talking to me then, however, if you would like to make it three days I can have you escorted out."

That comment seemed to almost trigger him as he tried to stop himself from getting agitated. He spoke in a flat tone and his face didn't change at all but I could tell it had really affected him."Are you really trying to upset me again? Or are you just that oblivious to what you're saying? If I'm being honest there's really not much of a difference when you're always making me so damn angry."

"I'm simply stating a fact. I won't be here on the weekends, and I am saying that if you do not want to speak with me it's okay, I can have you go back to your room now."

He stared at me in silence for a moment before he looked away and spoke with such venom that it was clear it wasn't just any random threat. "And do you really think I won't take you up on that offer? It's just another threat anyway. If I had my way, I wouldn't speak to you ever again." Then he laughed, but that laugh wasn't a lighthearted laugh, it was a laugh filled with sarcasm and malice. He was definitely trying to upset me with this statement as well.

"Oh. So now you want a different psychiatrist?" I questioned.

He rolled his eyes and shrugged, trying to stay cool despite everything I have said so far. "I'd probably prefer someone who actually knows what they're doing. You definitely are not it."

I grab the transfer paperwork behind my desk and start filling it out. "I mean if this is what you really want I will respect how you feel Archer. I will say, I am quite hurt, however. It's not every day I open up to my patients that I have murdered like I did with you. I thought we connected a bit, but I assumed wrong."

When I started filling out the transfer paperwork, he seemed to get even angrier, but at this point, his anger wasn't surprising. All the while he was glaring at me, his expression was full of anger and disappointment. He looked away for a brief moment before he spoke again. "We *did* connect. You're the first person I've found myself opening up to in years. But that does not change the fact that you're just as useless as all the past psychologists I've met."

I pause on my writing. "Does this me you still want a transfer? I could rip the paper up right now and forget this all happened." I stated.

Archer paused for a moment, he wasn't sure what to do right now. Did he really want to transfer or not? On one hand, I wasn't really helping him. On the other hand, he had started opening up to me in a way he hadn't in a long time. He then decided to look me in the eyes and spoke to me once again."Can I ask you a question?"

"Of course."

"If I were to stay, would you promise to not strike nerves every session? Like take a break in between sessions or something? The truth is I like talking to you, you're the only person I can trust in this whole entire place. Would you do that for me?"

I smiled and answered honestly. "I promise to try my best."

His face softened somewhat when I said that, he seemed to relax a little bit and he nodded his head. For a moment, he just sat there in silence, but then a smile spread across his face. He felt relief when he heard my answer. It was like he was finally getting the help he needed. He continued to stare at me and the smile just got bigger."Thank you. I truly mean that."

"Unfortunately, all this bickering caused us to waste time and our session has come to an end. I will see you in two days Archer."

"Yeah, I guess it did." He looked at me in silence for a moment before he spoke once again. "And hey, thank you again. I'll see you in two days." He smiled just a bit and it was clear I was making some sort of progress with him, even if it was only little by little.

# CHAPTER 6

It was Saturday, I wasn't sure how I was going to spend my day. I had been so wrapped up in work I really had not made time for myself. I lay in bed for a little while before deciding to get up and go to the nearby coffee shop. I was craving an iced caramel coffee. I jogged to the coffee shop down the road to see Johnathan, my boss there.

Johnathan was sitting at a table outside, sipping at his morning coffee and he looked up when I approached him, he had a smirk on his face which showed he wasn't surprised to see me. I smiled at him, "stalk me much."

"What can I say, I always notice when my employees are here and you're always so nice to look at." He smirked as he took another sip of his coffee and he seemed to be in a very good mood.

"Thank you, sir, for the compliment."

"You're welcome." He nodded his head before he paused and asked me a question. "So, how did your appointment with Archer go yesterday?"

I smiled at him. "It went swell."

"It did? I'm surprised, you usually leave him angry. I thought you guys got into another argument. What did you guys do to have such a good session?"

"We simply just communicated."

He thought for a good minute as he sipped his coffee again. "Really? You made the most progress with him by just doing nothing and talking like normal? That's it?"

I smiled. "I took your advice and it worked." I lied. I couldn't tell him the truth or else he would remove me from being his shrink.

He smiled, "Well, I am glad that you took my advice. I am the professional after all, I know what I am talking about." He said, arrogantly. He paused in between his sentences. "May I ask you a question?" His tone seemed, curious.

I nodded my head.

"This may come off as inappropriate, however, I find you really attractive. Would you want to go on a date with me next Saturday?" He asked, slightly smiling.

I was stunned. I have only been working here for a week, and he has only shown concern twice, the whole time I have been here. I cleared my throat. "Sir, I only just started to work here, barely a week ago. I am still getting to know everyone in the building. I don't think it is smart to move on quickly in our relationship. I also just moved here there is still so much for me to discover and people as well. Why, we are only mere acquaintances, not even friends yet. Shall we build our friendship up before we even think about dating?" I did not want to hurt him, however, I also was not attracted to him in that way.

He smiled, yet he looked defeated. "Of course, I am sorry if I made you uncomfortable. I will try not to get too ahead of myself next time."

I tilted my head, "It's okay. Baby steps. That is all I am asking." I said with a confident smile. The rest of the morning coffee was peaceful. We got to know each other for a little bit before he needed to return home. I returned home shortly after he did and spent my weekend soaking in bubble baths and watching movies. I hoped that my next working days would not be as awkward as I feared them to be. The weekend came to a quick end and tomorrow was Monday.

Archer was escorted back to my office and was strapped down in his chair. He was in a better mood today it seemed as if he was grinning from ear to ear when he saw me walk in. He then spoke to me before I could even say anything.

"I wanna try something this session. Let's just talk like normal, talk about anything we want. I know it sounds weird, but I don't want you to bring up anything about my issues. I just want to make a good connection with you before we get deep in my feelings again."

I nodded. "Okay. What shall we talk about?"

He took a moment to think of the first topic that came to mind and then he seemed to get an idea. "How about our interests? Do you have any hobbies or anything that you like to do in your free time? We can start with that."

I pondered the question over. The truth is I loved many things, I just never had time for any of them. "I would say music. I love playing guitar."

"That's interesting, I didn't know you could play the guitar. Who's your favorite artist? What kind of music do you usually like to play?"

"I don't normally play other's music, I like to write my own when I have time."

"Oh, you write your own music?" He raised an eyebrow, he never expected me to be one to write my own music. "That's quite cool. So, you compose the music, write the lyrics, and everything?"

"Yes, I do. What are your hobbies?"

He didn't really have any hobbies, but he wanted to keep the conversation going for as long as possible, so he lied."I like to draw. I'm not a *professional* artist or anything like that, I just draw on my free time when I want to unwind. It's a nice relaxing way for me to just let my mind run free."

"Ah, would you draw something for me?"

He hesitated for a moment before he spoke, he was clearly a bit embarrassed."Sure, I guess I could do that. What do you want me to draw?"

"Anything." I motioned the doctors to free him from his binds and hand him a pencil and paper.

"Alright, so basically anything goes." His mind was racing, trying to think of what he could draw to impress me. He was thinking something romantic, but that was a little bit too soon. He then finally decided on what to draw and he chuckled. "I got it. Just, one question, I don't mean to be inappropriate, but do you have a significant other?"

I chuckled a bit at his question. "No, I do not."

That made him relieved as he could have drawn something a little bit inappropriate. But then he remembered that I did ask for* anything *so he decided to ask me another questio n."And does romance make you feel uncomfortable? Like, do you mind if the drawing is a little intimate?"

"No, I don't mind," I was curious to see what he would draw me.

He smirked, that was good, he would definitely draw something that I would love. With a smirk on his face, he took the pencil and quickly but carefully got started on the drawing. He had started with the outline and now he was carefully shading in the drawing, I could tell he was taking this drawing very seriously. After about 15 minutes he stopped what he was doing and sat back, taking a second before speaking.

"I do have a question before I continue with the drawing. This drawing is just for you right? You won't show it to anyone else?"

"Of course. It is for my eyes only."

That was exactly the answer he was hoping to hear, that was good. He continued to shade, the drawing was almost complete. After 10 minutes he finished off the last bit of shading and he spoke up once again."Just to get another confirmation, you aren't going to tell anyone about this drawing, right?"

I laugh slightly. "I will not show or tell anyone."

He smirked and nodded his head as he put the pencil away before speaking again."Then may I ask you one last thing?"

"Of course."

He took a moment to think of what he was gonna ask me before speaking again. "Would you mind…could you keep this drawing with you? Just so you can keep it since it's for your eyes only?"

I nodded. "I will keep it in my purse."

He smiled once again and a small chuckle escaped his lips. "Good, good. Then I think I'm done with the drawing. Do you want to see it now?"

"Yes, yes I do."

He pulled the drawing out and showed it to me, it was of me. It was a very detailed drawing of me, every single one of my features was perfectly drawn. He had even drawn every little detail, including the small crease that I have next to my eyes. The drawing was just perfect.

"Archer, this is beautifuL" I was in complete awe.

He smiled as he watched my reaction, he was genuinely proud of the drawing and it showed as he spoke again."So, it lives up to your expectations? I know you said I can draw whatever I want, but I wanted to make this as special as possible for you. Do you recognize the facial expression I gave you?"

"I'm smiling. Why did you make me smile in your drawing?"

He chuckled slightly as he saw the puzzled look on my face."I just wanted it to be as special as possible for you. Your smile is one of the most beautiful things I have ever seen. So I just wanted to make sure that the drawing had an expression you would recognize but with the most adorable one at the same time."

Was he flirting with me? I cleared my throat noticing the time, I figured it was time to end the session before things got too serious. "Ah, it seems as if our session is up. I will see you in the morning."

He noticed that I probably didn't want to engage in that conversation anymore, and he didn't press the issue any further. He smirked as he saw the time as well."I guess it is. That drawing took me longer than expected, but it was worth it in the end. See you tomorrow as well."

As he was escorted out. My face was turning redder by the minute. I was completely flustered by this morning's session.

# Chapter 7

I woke up bright and early. I had a little extra time before work to analyze the picture Archer drew for me. It was the most beautiful drawing I had ever seen. I don't think I ever found myself pretty before, but in this drawing, I was....pretty. Before I knew it, time was ticking by fast and it was time to leave for work. I shoved the picture in my purse and headed off to work. When I arrived at work, there was a bouquet of roses on my desk and a card that read "From Johnathon." My boss really sent me flowers.  I rolled my eyes and noticed Archer sitting on the chair staring at me.

He was just silently watching me, that was until he started to speak."Are those flowers for you? And more importantly, who sent them?"

I smiled, I did not want to bring my personal life into business. "Just from an old friend," I stated.

He stared at me for a few moments before he raised an eyebrow and spoke again."Well, you are a beautiful woman, after all, it's no surprise that some friend would send you flowers. What's your friend's name by the way?"

"David." I lied.

He continued to stare at me, he seemed to think something was off. He then spoke once again. "How long have you known David?"

"He was an old high school friend. We are not here to discuss my friends, we are here to talk about you. How are you today?"

He shrugged, he still couldn't get over the fact that I was lying to him, but he decided to drop the subject. He took a deep breath as he sat up straight in his chair and sighed. "Well, I'm doing a little bit better today. But if you really want to talk about my feelings then I really want to talk to you about something first."

"Okay?"

"Do you remember that drawing that I made for you?"

"Yes."

"Can I ask you to do something for me?"

"Like what?"

"Well, because I gave you a gift, I figured why not give me a gift? I want better food options and less security around me."

I stared at him, not knowing what to say. I was stunned. "Giving you better food I can do, however the less security will be more tricky."

He smirked when I said that I would give him better food, but I noticed how his smirk quickly disappeared when I started talking about his less-security request. "Tricky? That doesn't sound too promising. Can't you just make it happen?"

"You are a known murderer. I don't think they can just 'give you less security.'"

"Come on, it's not like I kill people every day. And plus, they know that I'm willing to talk about my issues. I'm not a threat to anyone here anymore."

"In my eyes, you were never a threat. In their eyes, they see 23 dead shrinks."

"That was in the past! Everyone makes mistakes, and I'm no exception. Can't you just make it happen? I feel like I won't be able to open up and trust you again if we continue with this tight security."

"I feel like you are trying to manipulate me Archer," I state in a weary tone.

He laughed. "Oh come on, is there a problem using a little bit of manipulation? It's not like it harms you in any way, plus I already gave you a gift and there's nothing wrong with you giving me one in return."

I sighed, but a curious question came to my head. "What else would you manipulate me for?"

He smiled as he thought of every possibility that he could manipulate me. "I have a long list, but just a few would probably be getting better treatment or being able to get my way with things more often. Maybe if I get to know you a bit better there might be other methods I could use on you."

"Would you manipulate my heart?"

He smirked slightly as he got to the most interesting part of his list. He stayed silent for a while until he finally answered my question. "Who knows? That would actually be a very good method to use on you. That method will work if I play it right."

"Would you make me fall in love with you?"

He chuckled. "Of course, I could do that, that would be a very easy thing for me to do. I could get you to fall in love with me in a matter of days."

"Well, it's been a week and I haven't fallen in love. Do you think that if you tried to manipulate me into falling in love with you, you would end up falling in love with me?"

He smirked, the challenge was too tempting to not try. He really wanted to see if he could make me fall in love with him. He spoke with a smirk on his face. "That's an interesting question. I mean, I was gonna try to make **you** fall in love with **me**, but I guess it wouldn't be bad if I fell in love with you instead or if it ended up being both of us falling in love."

"And what if I don't fall in love?"

He kept his smirk throughout the entire time I spoke. "Hmm, I don't know. I've never failed before. So it would be a first if it ended up happening. Do you want me to try anyway? If so, I'm sure I could make you fall in love with me."

I leaned onto the table and looked at him. "I'm not easily fooled, I don't think you could successfully complete that challenge."

He stared back at me with a smirk, the challenge was getting more exciting for him. "Ohhh, a challenge. This just got a whole lot more interesting. Do you think you're unbreakable? That's it, I'm going to make this my goal to make you fall in love with me."

"Give it your best shot."

He smirked and leaned back on his chair, he finally had a new goal for his treatment. The challenge of making me fall in love with him was exciting, he loved it. A part of him almost wished that he failed, because he was curious as to what would happen if he were to actually fall in love. This is going to be such a fun week. "How long should this period of time be? A week, two weeks, or until you fall in love?"

# Chapter 8

The next day was filled with excitement. Archer had given himself a week to get me to fall in love. I had received a text from my boss asking me to meet up for dinner for casual chatting. I was not particularly excited, however, I did suggest we try to become friends and I am assuming this is his attempt.

I got ready for work and headed out the door. I walked into my office to see a free Archer sitting down, twirling a pen in his hand waiting for our session to begin.

He smiled when he saw me walk into the room, today was the day that he was planning on starting to try to make me fall in love with him. As he saw me take a seat in my chair, he took note of how my hair was tied up neatly with the occasional strands of hair poking out. He noticed how my cheeks were slightly flushed, I was definitely looking good today. "Good morning, today is going to be another delightful day as usual right? It's like we're finally starting to make some progress."

I laughed because I could see right through him and see how sarcastically cheerful he was while trying to make his point. "It is delightful, Archer. How are you feeling today?"

He smirked as he heard my laugh, I certainly was very smart. I could see right through him, but he liked that because that would make the challenge a little bit tougher. He wasn't going to let me know how he was feeling, but he did have one question for me as he sat up straight in his seat and spoke with a calm tone. "By the way, can you answer a question that I have?"

"I can try."

He paused for a moment and he took a deep breath before speaking again. "Do you happen to have a boyfriend or some-one special in your life? I know this may seem a bit out of the blue, but lately, I have been curious to ask you these types of questions."

I laughed because I had already answered this when he drew the picture of me. "No, I do not."

He laughed at my chuckle. I still managed to surprise him at times, even though I already told him.

"I see, that's good to know. Now I don't have to worry about a potential love rival." He smirked slightly at me.

I raised an eyebrow. "Just because I don't have a lover doesn't mean others are not interested in me. I actually had someone ask me on a date tonight. So it seems that you might have a potential love rival." I smiled with satisfaction.

Archer gasped in surprise as his face went slightly red. "Wait, someone asked you on a date? Oh boy, I see a potential problem. Well, may I ask who it is? Also, it's just a date or are you thinking of actually going on the date?"

"I will not reveal his identity. However, I was not going to go on the date but if it makes your challenge slightly harder, then I suppose I must go on this date."

Archer's face was still slightly red, he was getting irritated at the thought of me going on a date with another guy, especially if that man was an unknown entity. "Yeah, no. I think I'd like a name. Plus, how am I supposed to compete if I don't even know who this other guy is? I wouldn't be surprised if he was some hot model or something. You can't just go on a date with him while I'm here, trying to make you fall in love with me."

"Ah, jealous are we? Well, while I can't give you the name, I can tell you he is FAR from a model. He is a doctor of some sort."

He was still getting slightly annoyed at the idea of me going on a date, he really wanted to know who this guy was. When I told him that he was far from being a model, he was relieved. He smirked once again. "Okay, at least he's not a model. But he's not a threat, right? Like I don't have anything to worry about, or do I?"

"I guess I will find out after my date with him."

He laughed at my answer, at least I was honest."The good news is that you're being straightforward and honest, the bad news is that I still have to compete with some random doctor. But I'll win in the end. Just give me some details, do you even know if he's your type or are you just going to go on a date with him just be spiteful towards me?"

"What if it's a little bit of both?"

He scoffed and rolled his eyes."Wow, you really are a difficult woman. Do you even know what your type is? And are you really going to date this guy just to piss me off? Is that what you're going for here?"

"How about I tell you what I think my type is to give you some leverage?"

He raised an eyebrow as he leaned forward in his chair, he was curious to know what my type was.

"Alright, I'm listening."

"While I like my man to listen and be thoughtful, I also like them to have an insane side. I like them to know what fun is and let loose. I also like them to be jealous. As you can tell my type is toxic, yet loving."

My type was everything he imagined it to be so far. "Well, it seems like I fit your criteria pretty well. I mean, not only am I insanely jealous right now, but I'm also very toxic as well. However, I'm also very caring in my own way and I also know how to have a lot of fun. Maybe I'm your type after all."

"Ah yes, but you have one thing that I just can not love."

He cocked his head to the side, curious as to what that thing is that I supposedly cannot love. "What is that thing? I'm curious to hear your answer."

"You are my patient. It is unprofessional to grow love for a patient, in a romantic way of course."

He smiled, I certainly did have my limits. He had a feeling that he was going to make me break that limit soon. "I understand completely, but what about when I'm not your patient anymore? Would you consider falling in love with me if I wasn't your patient?"

"You will be my patient until you kill me, or this place kills you. But I have a feeling that even the whole doctor-patient relationship won't stop you from trying to do something."

He smirked and replied back with a sarcastic tone."Well, I do love a little bit of challenge. I do want to ask an innocent question though, would you ever consider taking me out on a date if I wasn't your patient? Let's pretend this whole doctor-patient relationship thing never existed. This is a strictly hypothetical question."

"And in this hypothetical situation are you still a murderer?"

"Hmm, in this hypothetical situation, I wouldn't have committed any murders and I'd be a law-abiding citizen."

"Then I suppose I would consider it," I smirked.

He smirked along with me. "Interesting, that's something I didn't expect you to consider. It's quite amusing how you could picture yourself going on a date with me. However, I have a feeling that you're going to find out sooner or later that it's very easy for me to break your limits. So how about we make this hypothetical date a little more interesting?"

"Let's hear it."

He smirked as he leaned forward in his chair. "If I'm able to convince you to go on a date with me and make you fall in love with me in the next week, would you agree to go on a date with me while we are still doing sessions here?"

"I don't want to spoil the future so we will just have to see. Our session has ended for today however and I must not be late to my date now."

He paused for a moment, a feeling of disappointment suddenly filled his body, but he had an important quest ahead of him.

"Right, right. I wish you luck on your date. I'll see you tomorrow at the usual time."

With that, he was escorted back to his room. I had packed an extra pair of clothes to go meet my boss at the diner. When I arrived he was not there yet so I grabbed a table and sent him a message to know I was already there. A few minutes passed by and he came to the table apologizing for being late.

"I'm so sorry, I had some paperwork to finish up." He explained.

"It's no worries. How was today?"

"It was boring. Filing out the same paperwork over and over. However, I do have a question for you." He asked in a serious tone.

"Ask away."

"One of my doctors overheard you and Archer's conversation. Something about you falling in love with him?"

"Ah, Archer has this idea that he could get me to fall in love with him. If that's what he thinks and it gets him to open up to me, then I shall let him believe it for now. However, this is a casual dinner. I do not want to talk about work."

He sighed. "I just want you to be careful, but yes we shall not talk about work. Do you want to drink?" He asked.

I am not much of a drinker, but one drink couldn't hurt. "Sure," I said with a smile.

He ordered us some alcohol and we drank and talked the night away. I got to learn that he came from a small town and grew up on a farm. At first, he wanted to become a veterinarian, but seeing his mom go insane and have no one to help her is what inspired him to be the doctor he is now. I was shocked and saddened by this news. Time flew by and before we knew it, it was time for our dinner to end. He offered to drive me home. I had walked after work to save on gas. I obliged and he dropped me off. "I will see you at work tomorrow Freya."

I smiled and waved him off. I was absolutely exhausted, so I headed to bed. It didn't take long for me to fall asleep.

# Chapter 9

The next day comes and I wake up feeling fresh. The strange thing is, I had a date with my boss last night, but I can't stop thinking about Archer. I find myself excited to see him, he keeps me loving work. I may not love him, but am I attracted to him? Yes, I am. I can find my patients attractive, so don't judge me there. I just can't love them.

I walk into my office beaming with happiness.

He looked up at me as I entered the room, he couldn't help but notice that I was beaming with happiness. "Ah, I can't help but notice the bright glimmer in your eyes. How was the date? I imagine that you had a good time right?"

I smiled at him. "Something like that."

He smirked and leaned back on his chair. "Oh, I see, you had an amazing time. You're really making me jealous you know... I haven't seen you this happy since you've been here. But hey, this is a good thing and I'm glad you enjoyed yourself. It proves that I also don't have to worry about a potential love rival."

"And why would you assume that you don't?"

He smirked, I certainly was giving him a hard time now. "Well, you didn't exactly tell me about him. You never gave him a name, so I can only assume that he isn't somebody who I need to worry about. So, is my assumption right?"

I rolled my eyes at his assumption. "Or it might just be someone I can't talk about. Maybe that very person works in this building with me?"

His eyes widened slightly, he was starting to get the feeling that he might see some competition soon. He was curious about who the mystery man was. "Oh, you're starting to make things interesting now. But who exactly is that person then? Am I at least able to describe what he looks like?"

"Who do you think it might be?"

He had a feeling that he already knew who this guy was, but he had to play along. "Well, I'm going to take your little hint in the form of a question. Do I know him? Have I met him before?"

"You might have met him. Yes."

He thought about all of the people that he'd met in this building and eventually decided that there was only one person he thought could be the mystery man. "This might be a little bit of a stretch, but is it... Dr. Maddox?"

"Are you referring to my boss? Johnathan Maddox?"

He nodded his head with a smug look on his face. "Yeah, your boss. So I was right, was I not? He's the mystery man?"

"And why would you assume that?"

Another smug smile appeared on his face. "Well, isn't it obvious? He is someone you can't talk about, and he definitely fits the description of your type. You might just be trying to be vague because you don't want to tell me out of fear that I might become jealous."

"If I am strict about keeping my relationship with you to just business, why wouldn't I be just as strict with my boss?"

He paused for a moment and looked at me, realizing that I had a good point. However, he's not going to admit that. "Hmmm, you're right. Well then, who else could it be then? You told me that the guy worked in this building, so who else fits those criteria?"

"I said he MIGHT work here. What if I was just trying to throw you off?"

He smiled as he laughed at my counterattack. "Ha, not bad. But you can't keep giving me hints like this and not expect me to figure out who the love rival is. The fact that you're being secretive and vague about his identity is proof that you're hiding something. But I'll play along, who do you suppose this love rival could be then?"

"But then again, I could not be trying to throw you off." I shrugged. "I guess we will never know."

He smirked."If you're not trying to throw me off, then you wouldn't be so secretive about this guy. I get the feeling that I'm starting to get close to finding out who this mystery man is. I might have to up my game if I want to beat him to win your heart. So just how secretive are you going to be?"

"As secretive as one can get."

He chuckled. "It's almost funny how vague you're being about this guy. You know, it's okay to just tell me who it is, don't make this any harder than it already is. The curiosity is killing me, so just who exactly is this mystery man that's stealing all of your attention?"

"What if there is more than one?"

He raised an eyebrow as it looked like he had finally trapped me. This should be interesting. "Oh, so there are actually multiple men who are after you now? You must really be popular with the guys. I'm gonna have to start planning for multiple dates then. But how many are there? Do you think that you're getting a lot of love and attention from all of these men right now?"

"But then again, there might only be one?"

He chuckled, this was really a game and a half with me.

"Oh, so there might only be one guy? Or are you just trying to keep me on my toes? Let me guess, you're going to keep being vague now right?"

I just smiled.

He let out an exaggerated groan. "God, you're making this extremely hard. I mean, I don't mind working extra hard for your love, but it seems like you're not making this easy for me at all. I think you're enjoying challenging me, but I will find out who this love rival is. I'm sure of it."

"You just making toying with you so easy."

He smirked, I really was good at this whole challenging thing. "Well, I gotta admit, you're doing a really good job at keeping me on my toes. The curiosity is really building up inside of me though, and trust me I do not tolerate curiosity well. In fact, I've been thinking of a way to make you crack and tell me the man's identity."

"Do tell."

He smirked as an idea came to his head. "Alright, I think I know something that would make you crack. Tell me, did you enjoy your date last night?"

"It was fine."

He chuckled and rolled his eyes. "Well, that's just a blatant lie, you're being extremely vague again. You're hiding a lot of truth from me, I can tell by the tone in your voice and how your body language changed when you answered that. It sounds like you really enjoyed the date."

"I enjoyed our conversation, yes."

Archer's face was still smirking as he let out a loud laugh. "Wow, you're such a bad liar, and I absolutely love it. It's so obvious that you're lying to me. So you're telling me that my love rival is some smooth talker that makes you laugh, huh?"

"Who said our conversations were romantic?"

He laughed, I had another very good counterattack. "Well, I'm assuming it was just a friendly date? I mean, it's a bit of a stretch to think that you went out on a date with another guy and it wasn't a romantic date."

"And if it was a friendly date?"

He smirked before replying. "If it was a friendly date then I wouldn't feel as threatened by the thought of this other guy. In other words, I wouldn't mind as much if it was just a friendly date. Because if it was a romantic date, then that means he did something that I haven't been able to do so all this time, which is making you feel some type of way. If it was just a friendly date where he made you laugh then at least I know he didn't manage to do anything special."

"Who said it made me feel any type of way? Also what if the friendly date was just to build our friendship so it could turn into something romantic?"

An amused smile crossed his face as the curiosity was building back up within him again. "So the date was intended to only be friendly? What makes you say this date was intended to build your friendship in the hopes of making it something romantic? If the date was just to build your friendship, could it have been possible that you two got a little bit too close and ended up flirting and/or having a romantic evening?"

"We did get close, actually."

He chuckled, I was making this way too easy for him. He could literally feel his eyes gleaming with joy as he heard that we got close during my 'date'. "How close? Did you two hold hands? Did you two get a little touchy? If you two got a little too close then that would be very amusing to me."

"Not physically no, but emotionally we did."

He smirked, he couldn't believe that this was actually happening. "So this date really did affect your emotions. The thought of another guy affecting your emotions like that, it's really amusing to me. I guess my job is really going to be even harder than I originally thought." He laughed a bit as he paused and gave a sly look at me. "So you're basically admitting that this other guy has been able to win you over emotionally."

"Maybe not win me over, but pique my interest slightly."

His smirk broadened as he chuckled. "Well, that's still saying something. So this guy has managed to pique your interest huh? Would you say that this peak is significant, or is it just small enough for me to still beat him? You must really be enjoying our little games because I'm definitely enjoying this now."

"I guess you would just have to find out."

"I guess I will just have to find out then. I can already tell that this guy is definitely going to be a big challenge for me. So tell me then, what about this other guy that you met that made him spark your interest? Did he have some sort of talent or skill?"

"To be honest. He asked me to be his girlfriend. I rejected him and told him I would like to get to know him a bit better before we make that kind of move on each other."

He let out a deep breath, his curiosity was building up once again. He wanted to know more about this mysterious man. "Well, I'm going to try to keep my emotions in check. It's quite amusing to find out that someone already managed to ask you to be his girlfriend, I'm actually impressed he got that far. So let me get this straight. You rejected him and told him that you wanted to get to know him better before you guys started dating? Was there any reason for that?"

"I don't just date people for looks. He is tall and handsome, however, it's the personality that really attracts me."

He chuckled as he leaned back on his chair once again. "Wait, so that means that this guy that met your standards was just good-looking, but not attractive in personality? So he basically met the standard for your looks criteria, but in personality, he did not. So does that mean that you're looking for someone who fits both criteria, personality, and looks?"

"I am still learning his personality. However, our session is up for the day."

"Well, I guess you're right. You know, our sessions are ending way too quickly for me. So how are you ever going to fall in love with me if you aren't giving me time to get to know you? I was hoping for a little longer today just in case I could find a weak spot in your defenses, but instead, it just gave me a bit more information to piece together. Well, I suppose I've got my work cut out for me. I will continue to find out more about you and this other guy."

"Goodbye Archer."

He rolled his eyes as he replied."Don't even get me started with that goodbye, we both know that we're going to see each other again. Until next time."

I laughed and he was escorted out. I went home, exhausted for the day. When I got home I noticed a strange car parked outside my home, I brushed it off assuming it was my new neighbor.

# CHAPTER 10

I woke up to another message from my boss, he was asking for another friendly date tonight. I messaged him back and said that we could do that. I walked outside to still see that strange car, it had driven off when I noticed it, strange. I disregarded to car and headed off to work.

I walked into my office to see Archer pacing my office back and forth.

He stopped pacing and looked over at me. His expression changed to a playful smirk. "Well, well. Look who's back. It seems like somebody got here quite early. You're not too excited to see me now, are you? Because I know you were always excited to see me at the beginning of our sessions."

I rolled my eyes at his statement. "Quite confident this morning are we?"

He chuckled. "Why yes, yes I am. As a matter of fact, I'm feeling quite confident today. I even have a plan to make you crack."

"Oh?"

His smirk broadened as he continued speaking with a confident tone. "It seems that every other plan I have with you has failed me so far, but I'm pretty certain that this plan won't fail. In order to make you crack and finally tell me who this guy is, I just need to use a little bit of... psychological warfare."

"Continue," I state amused. I walk over and sit in my chair.

He smirked as he replied. "Gladly. Psychological warfare is a powerful tool when it comes to breaking down someone's barriers. It has the capability of pushing someone's buttons and manipulating their beliefs. I can use this tool to find and push the right buttons to get you to tell me who this mystery man is. And I have done plenty of research on the subject of Psychological warfare to perfect my craft, so be prepared for your defenses to be broken."

"I think I am prepared thus far."

He chuckled to himself as he saw that I wasn't taking this seriously. "Good, being confident is the first step to getting broken. Do you really think you can stand your ground against some Psychological warfare? Let me just ask you this: How confident are you in your defenses?"

"Very."

He smirked. "Well now, I guess I have no choice, but to see just how confident you believe in your defenses. So here's what I'm going to do, I have to ask you one question and you have to answer it truthfully or else your defenses will be broken."

"Okay."

He smirked, feeling pretty confident in this moment as he spoke carefully. "Alright, the question is this: Are you attracted to me? Do you actually find me attractive and have romantic feelings for me?"

"I do find you attractive. However, how is the Psychological warfare? And wouldn't you try to win me over with moves instead of trying to waste your time to find out how this mystery man is?"

He let out a loud laugh, he had me right where he wanted me. This was going just as planned. "Well now, I think I've found my chink in your armor. You must actually have some feelings for me if you find me attractive, and I'm pretty certain that you're attracted to me because of my handsome features and charm. I guess this makes it even more amusing that you're attracted to some other guy who's probably not half as good as me."

"You know what I think?"

The smirk still remained as he replied. "Why don't you tell me what you think? I'm intrigued."

"I think the reason why you are so focused on this mystery man is because you are too scared to make a bold move on me, unlike him."

His smug expression faded as he heard this thought out loud. Maybe this little game wasn't as pointless as he thought it'd be. I was making valid points, and that thought actually worried him. "Are you saying that I haven't been making any bold moves towards you at all? You seriously believe that?"

"I feel like you have said some bold things, but actions-wise. You just sit there."

He chuckled, that statement was quite true. He actually hasn't made much of an effort towards me. He has definitely shown me attention and said some bold things, but he hasn't really gone out of his way to truly charm me. "You know, that's actually a really good point. I know that you actually love it when guys make bold moves like that. I should actually start doing more of that."

"So what's your first big bold move, Archer? It can't be asking me on a date seeing that you're not allowed to leave this place."

He chuckled as he thought up a first bold move. He was definitely going to make me crack soon, so he had to come up with a good one. He knew he couldn't ask me out on a date since he wasn't allowed to leave the facility, but it didn't mean he couldn't do something that was just as bold and charming. "Well, how about I do something to really show you how much I truly care about you? It might be something little, but it also might have a big impact on our relationship."

"Go for it."

It was time. Time to make his first big bold move. It's now or never. He walked over to me, his face close to mine as he spoke in a firm tone. "Close your eyes."

I closed my eyes, intrigued at what he was going to do.

I could hear the subtle sound of him approaching me. My heart immediately started pounding in my chest as the butterflies in my stomach were going crazy. His lips were almost touching mine as his voice spoke in a firm and demanding tone. "You're gonna keep those eyes closed until I tell you to open them, understand?"

I nodded.

He continued to move his lips closer and closer, his breath was hot on my skin as his lips were only inches away from mine. I felt the subtle smell of his minty breath, even the subtle sound of his lips moving would keep me on the edge of my seat. I could feel his hands move to wrap around my waist and his fingers caress the soft skin underneath and even my hips. Then his body was pressed against me and I felt him get even closer to my body. And finally, his lips were only centimeters away from mine as he finally began to speak. He was only going to tease me but not give me the actual kiss. At least not right now, he was going to wait a little bit longer. "Can I ask you something important before I tell you to open your eyes now?"

"Yes."

He slowly pulled away from me, his face still close to mine as his lips were still just barely touching mine. He took a deep breath before speaking. "So, would you have been fine if my lips actually had touched yours? Would you have been ready to kiss me if I had started to kiss you right now?"

As much as I really wanted to kiss him, I knew that I couldn't, it was unprofessional. So I didn't answer. I wanted to be honest, but I could not answer him at that moment.

He kept his face close to mine as he waited for the answer, but all he got was silence. He didn't even care that I didn't answer, he knew it to be true. He chuckled, I was being shy. He was actually enjoying this a little too much as I seemed extremely flustered. But he knew exactly how to take advantage of this moment."I'm going to take that as a yes. Since you didn't respond that just means you don't want to admit it. Right?"

Again. I didn't answer. I opened my eyes and stared directly into his.

He continued to smirk and looked directly into my eyes as he spoke. "You can try as hard as you want but you're not lying to me. I know my kiss would've felt really good had it landed on those beautiful lips of yours. I can tell that you want me badly. Just the thought of my lips touching yours has you feeling some type of way."

I backed up and looked the other way flustered. I really wanted his kiss, but I couldn't. "I.. I think it's time our session ended today."

He let out a small chuckle as he spoke, I was so damn predictable. My actions spoke louder than words, and his little game is going far too well. "Aww, already running away? What about the fact that I still want to know who your little mystery man is?"

"I'm not running away!"

He smirked and took a step closer to me, I just couldn't resist him and he knew this damn well. "Yes, you are. You're backing away from a possible kiss and trying to avoid any discussion of your mystery man. You can pretend all you want but I've already seen through all of your defenses."

I looked down at the ground, and for once I was completely speechless.

He giggled, as his smirk widened on his face. He loved the fact that he had me backed up into a corner like this. "I can read you like a damn book. Every move of yours has been predictable. You're attracted to me and you can't resist my charm. However, you're also attracted to someone else."

But the truth was, I wasn't attracted to someone else. I was trying to force myself to be so I had a distraction from Archer. I couldn't let him know that though.

He smirked again, his expression seemed a little mischievous as he spoke.

"But you are not attracted to him. That's why you have been so vague, he is just a pawn. Well then, that's even more interesting. Now we know the real reason why you refuse to tell me who this mystery man is. Why don't you just tell me the truth now and let me get closer to you so I can give you that kiss you really want."

I shook my head, I can't.

He took a step closer again, his smirk only getting bigger and bigger with each step. He spoke with a firm tone, but he still managed to put some teasing into his voice. "Why not? You know the longer you resist the more I'm likely to be able to break you eventually."

"Let's just see how much you can break me then," I said with a smirk.

He smirked also, as he kept his gaze locked with mine as he leaned in a bit closer. "Well, now look at that confidence of yours. I bet you really think you're going to win this one, don't you? You know what, you could be right. Maybe you will win this one. I guess we can finally see what the hell happens when I try breaking down your defenses once and for all. Because I know I won't give up until I completely figure you out."

I smiled and had him escorted out of the room. "Until next time Archer."

He nodded and smirked, he was definitely not happy to leave me alone like this. The fact that he had to wait for next time was almost unbearable to him, he hated not being in control. "Well, it appears I won't be able to break you yet at least. I was hoping to pull it off today, but you're stronger than I thought. I guess I won't be seeing you for another 24 hours until our next session, huh?"

"24 hours."

He smirked a bit, I was going to take it that literally instead of making this moment last. I guess I wasn't as weak as he initially thought I was. He hated this, the fact that a damn psychiatrist could keep him at bay and resist his charm. It was absolutely crazy. He nodded and replied. "Well, it's going to be a long 24 hours, that's for sure. But I'm patient, I'll wait."

# Chapter 11

After I got off work it was time to meet up with Johnathan. I really did not want to meet up with him, yes he is kind, but I just have this icky feeling in my stomach about building this false hope with him. I went home and got dressed in some casual clothing and then walked to the cafe down the street. He was already sitting there, he looked anxious and upset.

"Hey is everything okay?" I asked as I sat across from him.

"Are you and Archer doing anything inappropriate?" He asked.

I can't understand how he always knew something was up. "No. Why do you ask?"

He cleared his throat, he could clearly tell I was lying. "I was just checking in, that's all. I know, I know. No work talk."

I nodded my head and smiled. "Correct. So how was everything today."

"Well. I took off work today because I had some things to do, family business. Boring stuff." He explained while ordering us some coffee.

"Ah, well I hope everything is okay."

"You're too kind."

We spent the next hour talking. I told about how I grew up. My family was poor, they could barely afford to get me through school, and I had to pay for my college. Most of the time we hopped and hopped to different houses or apartments. I almost had to drop out of college because my mother fell ill, but she made a speedy recovery. I had two siblings, a brother and a sister, they still live at home with my parents. he showed compassion for my time growing up, however, I couldn't tell him the whole truth about my family.

I did kill my family, that is true. I murdered them because my father was a pimp. He sold women and as a child, I was one of those. I never went overseas and left my house, men would just pay him to take advantage of me. My mother encouraged it, but my siblings never suffered through it. The truth was I had no idea where my siblings were when I murdered my family, they were at my grandparents and I would assume they were still there. One night I just snapped, the cops knew who my parents were and simply turned a blind eye to everything, it was just easier that way.

We finished the night off with one last coffee before he took me home. I waved him off goodbye and he left. When I walked up to my door, there was a teddy bear and a note attached to it, "Until we meet again." I was confused but I had assumed Archer must have sent someone to do this, it was sweet.

The next morning came and it was right back to work for me. I jumped in my car and headed to work. When I walked in my office Archer was standing there waiting for me at the door.

He smiled when he saw me, and the smirk was back on his face. He seemed somewhat confident as he made his entrance. But he was still trying to figure out what my game was, I was a lot more tricky than he ever imagined. "Well, well. It looks like you weren't joking when you said 24 hours. Looks like someone is taking things very seriously. You look pretty in that outfit today. Did you make sure to dress nice just for me?"

"I have to dress nice for work, thank you though. However, I have a question."

He raised an eyebrow as he leaned against the wall behind him. "Yeah? What's this question of yours?"

"Did you leave a present at my door?"

He chuckled as he replied. "Leave a present at your door? Why the hell would I leave a present at your door?"

"I didn't know if that was part of your plan or not."

He looked confused. "Well of course it wasn't a part of my plan. Even if my goal is to break you down eventually, there's definitely no need for presents. It's just a waste of good money." He then laughed. "Besides, why the hell would I leave a present on your porch like some damn kid? I'm way too mature for that."

"Well. it would've worked. Oh well. I wondered who did leave that at my door then."

He chuckled again, I had him curious now. "Hm...someone left a present on your doorstep? Wonder who could've done that? Do you think someone has a crush on you?"

"Well, it couldn't have been the mystery man because we were on another date last night. So I am not sure."

He smirked and spoke in a teasing tone. "So, you still haven't told me who this mystery man is. Or how your date was. Was it a good one or...are you just wasting time with him?"

"That is none of your business," I stated while smirking. I knew it was getting to him.

His smirk didn't fade as he replied. "Fine, I'll let you keep that one as a secret, for now at least. But you have to admit, your little mystery man is getting annoying, you don't tell me anything about him. How could I possibly know what strategy to use to break you down if you don't tell anything about him?"

"Because secrets are fun."

He chuckled. "Well, you certainly know how to be annoying. It's also a pain in the ass for me because I have no idea how to get through your defenses with all this 'secret' crap going on. I'm guessing that's why you do it because you must have some feelings for this mysterious man."

"If that's what you want to believe. Our last sessions really haven't been therapeutic like they should be, so tell me how have you been?"

He let out a small chuckle as he replied casually. "Well, I've actually been fine. Nothing special. However, I'm not very happy about how this session has been so far. It's a lot harder to get through all these 'secrets' in your head to get to the core of which I can break you down. It's going to take a lot longer to get you to the point where I can actually start manipulating and controlling you the way I want to."

"Well, your week of trying to make me fall in love ends in 2 days, are you saying you are going to need more time? Or are you going to do another bold move?"

The small smirk that was present from earlier on in the session instantly faded. He was not going to admit that it might take him more time just to be able to get me to fall for him. He had to maintain his dominance. "No...that's not what I'm saying at all. You see...my bold move got a different reaction out of you than what I expected...but I do have one thing up my sleeves, I just have to think of the next move that could finally allow me to start getting this relationship where I need it to be."

"And what trick do you have up your sleeve?"

He smirked as he spoke. "All I'm going to say is that it's going to be another big bold move since that one didn't do what I expected it to, but it's going to be better than the first. I'm not going to let someone like you just stay stubborn with all your 'secrets' and 'mysterious man'. You'll show me where your weakness lies eventually, I just have to figure it out."

"Ah, I see." I chuckled. I was amused by his efforts.

He chuckled also. "And you know what? I really want to see how far I can take this, and how badly I can make you fall for me. I love a challenge, especially when it's one that involves breaking you down mentally. However, I'm not going to just say that right up front since I wouldn't want to show my hand too much."

"I'm still waiting to see this bold move of yours." I love testing him. Can't you see?

He smirked at me "Oh, I know you're waiting. But you're going to have to wait a little longer before I finally make my move. I'm still thinking about it, and I want to make sure it's just perfect. I have a few ideas running around in my head at the moment, but I haven't decided which one I want to use yet. I don't want to make a mistake when it comes to you."

"Well, you only have two days."

"Two days? That's plenty of time. I mean, it's not like the second the clock hits midnight and it's a new week, that means I'm automatically out of the race to have you love me, right? I could literally get the ball rolling at 11:59 PM if I wanted to. So I have plenty of time to come up with the perfect bold move for you."

"You sure do have a lot of confidence for a man that has a short period of time. Well if you are not going to do anything bold, should we just end the session here?"

He chuckled and smirked, he kept up his confident demeanor even though I saw through his bluff. "So now what? You want me to just sit back do nothing while you continue having dates with this mystery man of yours? Are you saying you don't even want to see me put my plan into motion?"

"To be quite frank with you, I don't think you have a plan. I think you just expected it to be as easy as snapping your fingers."

This had him amused as he laughed. He couldn't believe how far I had already gotten under his skin. It's as if all his little "mind games" weren't working as he thought it would. "That's true. I did expect all this to be easier than it is. You're a lot harder to figure out than I thought. I mean, I didn't even get the reaction I was hoping for when I pretended to kiss you earlier today. Now I have to rethink my next move."

"What reaction were you expecting?"

He smirked and replied. "I was expecting you to get more flustered than what you actually did. I was hoping that your cheeks would get redder than a tomato, and you'd turn away to prevent me from seeing you blush. But instead, you just kept looking right back at me. And I have to say that I was quite surprised. I expected that my charm was going to have you wrapped around my finger by now."

"Try a bolder move I supposed."

He smirked, he felt a bit insulted. He definitely didn't like the way I was speaking about him. "A bolder move than trying to kiss you? I could, but is that really what you want? A more bold move than the one I just tried? Or do you now want to see how bad this can get before we even get there?"

"Let's see how bad it can get."

# Chapter 12

He chuckled as he smirked, he was definitely liking the way this is going. He'd definitely have fun playing more mind games with me."Are you sure about that? Do you really want to see just how much this can get to before I can finally have you wrapped around my fingers? Are you really that persistent to see me fail?"

"I am."

He smirked, and for the first time today, I saw his genuine grin instead of the fake smirks he always carries."You are quite a persistent one I have to admit. But I am more than satisfied that you're eager to see just how bad this can get. I love playing these little mind games, and I really enjoy playing them with someone as smart and persistent as you are. You are definitely not going to be easy to break."

"For today, our session has ended, I hope you have something figured out. I will stop by later tonight for another session with you instead of forcing you to wait another 24 hours."

He was definitely a bit shocked that I was already planning for another session, but he wouldn't let me see that. He had to maintain his confidence at all times when dealing with me. Instead, he simply replied with a confident look in his eyes."Ah, I see. Well, I'll make sure I have something planned by later this evening. You won't regret it I promise."

With that, he was escorted away. I went home to take a nap before returning, however, when I arrived at my door another present was left there. It was a box of heart-shaped chocolates with a note. "I will see you again." I was starting to get a creepy feeling and tossed the chocolates away, I don't know who keeps leaving presents at my door. I made myself lunch and took an hour's nap. I was refreshed and ready to go in for another session. I walked into my office to see my boss in the office.

"Oh, hello there," I stated, surprised.

"Oh, hello. I thought you already had your session with Archer?" He asked.

"I did, but we had scheduled a second one today considering he had some more things he needed to discuss with me. Why are you in my office."

"Well, actually I wanted to talk to you about Archer. I had overheard he was sleeping with one of the nurses, I came to see if he had mentioned anything about that."

"Oh, no he has not."

"Well in your second session could you get a name? We don't tolerate things like that."

I nodded my head and he left, I asked for the doctors to have Archer brought back here, and I noticed that he had less security. I could only assume how he got that.

He was definitely caught off guard that his secret was found out. He figured he'd made sure that he was smart about hiding his affair. He tried his best not to let his surprise show, and he succeeded for the most part. As for the nurses that he was sleeping with, he had made sure that they understood that they weren't allowed to talk about this to anyone.

"So sleeping with a nurse was this trick up your sleeve?"

He seemed to get a bit annoyed that I had found out about his affair. But since I brought it up, he might as well be honest about it."Yes, it was. How did you know that I was sleeping with a nurse anyway?"

"I'm assuming one of the guards saw and reported it to my boss."

He rolled his eyes."Really? That is so annoying. I really thought I was doing a good job of keeping my affair secret. Now I have to figure out which guard it was so I can make sure to keep him out of the game." It's not like his affair meant much anyways, he was only using her for an easy lay. But he still didn't like the fact that someone had found out about it.

"Did you think sleeping with her would make me jealous?"

He smirked and laughed. He had to admit that was not a bad thought, one of the perks to his affair was definitely the potential in making me jealous. However, that wasn't his initial intention."Well..that was one of the outcomes I was aiming for. Yes. She's very beautiful, and I figured it would be hard for you not to be jealous."

"Well, it didn't." I was clearly lying.

He laughed once again."Oh really? I was really hoping it would work. I mean, she's extremely beautiful and she really knows how to use her body. You really should be jealous. I mean, just look at her in comparison to yourself. There's no comparison at all. I figured that would make you jealous that a woman like her was getting someone like me every night."

"I don't even know which nurse it is that you are sleeping with."

He let out another chuckle."Oh, so you're not jealous now because you don't know her face? But you can definitely see in your mind how beautiful she is, can't you? You can probably already see us together, her and me, making out and you just wishing it was you instead of her."

I scoffed. "Hardly."

He laughed at this. It was honestly really cute how hard I was trying to convince myself that I wasn't jealous. He was pretty convinced that I was extremely jealous right now, but there wasn't much he could do to prove it to me. Instead, he continued as if nothing had happened."Really? That's not what your jealousy is telling me. I can just see it in your eyes how badly you're wishing you were her."

"Well, does she mean anything to you?"

He was quite irritated that I wasn't falling for this, he really thought this would work. For some reason, I just seemed resistant to every move he has tried to make. He did manage to make me blush a few times during these sessions, but besides that, I had pretty much always resisted him."Does she mean anything to me? Of course not. She's just another pawn in my game, I couldn't care less about her. I'm just using her for an easy lay."

"Oh, how charming." I sarcastically commented.

He laughed and smirked."I should've known you'd say something like that. I just knew this trick wasn't going to work. I guess you're just going to have to watch me sleep with her while you sit there thinking about me every second. That must be killing you inside knowing that such a beautiful person is getting me every night."

I scoffed again. "You are quite full of yourself," I said while getting slightly irritated.

He smirked and laughed at my irritation. He quite liked this side of me. The anger was attractive. He couldn't help it. My irritation definitely made him feel even more confident in himself.* "Awh...is your pride hurt? Are you mad that I'm sleeping with someone way more beautiful than you?"

I was starting to get really pissed at this point, "Fuck you!"

He let out another loud laugh like he couldn't help it. I was finally finally starting to show some emotion. It was a bit satisfying."Your language, Freya. Your language."He then chuckled."So, have I finally pissed you off? Are you finally going to tell me whether or not you're actually jealous of my affair?"

"You know what. Two can play that game. I will sleep with my mystery man and I hope you think about every second of it. My skin touching his skin and NOT yours." I said while leaning into his face.

He started smiling and grinning the more I kept talking. He was definitely enjoying this right now.."Is that so? You're going to go sleep with your mystery man and try to distract yourself from me? Maybe you should use your mystery man as a substitute for me. Try to imagine it's me while you're with him. Although that's probably pretty hard, maybe you should get a picture of my face before you do the deed with him, just to make it more realistic."

"UGH. You can be so unbearable at times!" I screamed.

He chuckled, it was clear that he was enjoying how angry I was getting right now. He was definitely starting to really get a rise out of me."What? Am I hitting some buttons here? I mean, it is pretty hard to control yourself around me. But you're going to enjoy your night with your mystery man. I'll just go have fun with this gorgeous nurse of mine."

That was it. I was officially pissed. I raised my hand to slap him.

Once I raised your hand, a smirk came over to his face. This was what he was waiting for. He wanted me to get angry and he wanted me to hit him. My anger would make him feel more dominant and more controlling over me. A thought he was really starting to enjoy.He was waiting for me to slap him, he was looking straight at me and not taking his eyes off of me even though he knew the slap was coming. And he didn't try to dodge it, or even defend himself. He just stood there waiting.

I just groaned and turned the other way.

He let out a laugh as he smirked. "Well, seems like some-one is finally backing down. That's definitely a first. I really thought you were going to actually hit me right now. I'm disappointed, I was actually really hoping you were going to put your hands on me and show me just how mad you really are."

"It's not too late, don't test me." I seethed.

He smirked and replied in a playful tone."Is that so? Are you *really* going to hit me? I mean, I definitely don't think you have the guts to hit me. I don't think you are willing to put your hands on me. But if you think that'll make you feel better, you can go ahead and try, I won't stop you."

I stood up and marched my way over to him and slapped him hard across the face. "Oh look, for once you got what you wanted." I spat out.

His smile only grew bigger as he smirked and nodded his head."Yes! That's perfect. It's pretty damn hot when you get angry, you know? It makes you look so attractive when that side of you comes out. You should get angry with me more often."

I was just too angry to even respond back.

He liked seeing me this angry. He found my anger pretty hot. Even if it was only temporary anger. He had definitely hit a button when he had brought up his affair."You know, you have a really attractive way of showing your anger. Your fists, your facial expressions. It's sexy...It almost makes me tempted to do something that would piss you off just so I could see it again."

"Oh piss off."

He laughed, it was adorable seeing me like this. To think that I would allow myself to be so easily angered was a huge turn-on."Oh, come on, don't you think this is kinda fun? This tension between us is kind of amazing, you know? I like making you angry. You're so pretty when everything just finally comes out."

"Now what? Now that you got to see me like this what's next on your plan." I sarcastically said.

He had a hard time not laughing, this whole thing was incredibly amusing to him. The tension between the two of us was intense, there was this feeling that this would lead to something big at the very end of our sessions. He definitely liked the way this was going."Well, now I have everything exactly where I want it to be. You are angry. You are jealous. You're probably thinking about my affair right now every second. I like having you like this, it makes me feel dominant and control over you."

"Oh, that's it? You just did this to piss me off. You had no plan to swoop me off my feet after this? How pitiful."

He was pretty surprised by this, he wouldn't admit but I had a good point. He hadn't thought about what to do next. So far he had been focused on making me angry, but now that I was angry there was nothing he had prepared. He then realized that he might as well admit that he hadn't thought that far ahead."I..uh...yeah, you're right. I haven't thought about what comes next. But at least you're angry now, which was my goal."

"Well now I don't love you, I am just pissed at you."

He chuckled a little bit and rolled his eyes."Oh, don't pretend like you're not obsessed with me. Yes, you're angry and jealous but you've still been falling for my little tricks all this time. I mean, you did fall hard for the affair trick earlier. You seemed pretty worked up over that one, I'm going to enjoy playing with that for a while."

I just ignored him, he was arrogant and annoying.

He didn't seem to care that I was ignoring him. He felt powerful knowing that he had made me angry. He even felt an urge to take advantage of this anger and say something that was really bound to annoy me. He just couldn't resist playing with me right now. He was going to enjoy this little back-and-forth between the two of us."Oh come on, are you seriously going to ignore me now? I really thought you would be more tempted to talk to me after being so upset about my affair. What is going on in that pretty little head of yours?"

"Our session is over." I stormed out of the room and had the doctors take him back to his room.

He let out a chuckle once he saw me leaving. I seemed even more angry now than when I had slapped him. He felt pleased with himself, he liked being the one in control over me. He didn't really care that the session was over, he had accomplished what he had set out to do.That's when he finally realized that they were going to take him back. He hated that idea. He didn't want to go into his room, he didn't want me to leave because he didn't want this time between the two of us to end.

# Chapter 13

I woke up, not wanting to go to work this time. I dreaded it actually. He had broken me. I was exhausted from our argument yesterday. Nonetheless, I got ready and went to work, when I arrived, Archer was in the office with a worried expression.

Before I could even sit down he blurted, "Our sessions may be put on paused. for a bit."

I was confused. "Why so you can free time with that nurse of yours." I said sarcastically.

"No, because I killed her. They haven't found her body yet, but when they do, I will be put in solitary confinement."

I was in shock, I couldn't believe what he had said. He said all of this so casually, without even an emotional twitch. The way he said that he killed her was so relaxed and calm. As for that nurse, she was already dead? He just let it all spill out. He then chuckled a little. Was he being completely serious about her being dead right now? Was this just a joke? It was pretty hard to tell with him, he had such a deadpan expression.

"Well. Why did you kill her?"

He smirked as he shook his head slightly. It wasn't for me, unfortunately. But he did like the fact that I seemed at least a little bit interested in him after finding out about this."Oh, you really want to know why? I'm not sure if I should tell you. But I might as well, I have nothing to lose anymore anyways."

"I mean you were sleeping with her one day then the next you killed her, of course, I have questions."

He chuckled as he nodded his head."That's fair enough. Maybe I should start by asking you a question. Does this scare you? The fact that I just admitted to killing someone?"

"You are a murderer, I kind of expected it."

That was definitely a fair point."Yeah, I am a murderer. But I'm a murderer you were falling for, right? I mean, you were even jealous when I slept with her that night. But that didn't scare you away."

I scoffed. "'A murderer I'm falling for.' How arrogant."

He smirked. I was making it so easy for him. He enjoyed the way he could just pull my strings and make me feel a certain way. That little scoff gave him the satisfaction he needed."Oh, are you not falling for me? Because let me tell you, that jealousy was pretty obvious on your face. Your facial expressions are almost as easy to read as a book."

"You didn't answer my question. WHY did you kill her?"

He sighed, this is where things got complicated. He was going to have to reveal his motive eventually. And as much as he didn't want to tell me, he would eventually have to."Well, to put it simply. I killed her because she annoyed me. I just couldn't stand her presence and her constant attempts to make me 'behave.' You know, I really thought she would be able to 'fix' me, but her attempts were pathetic."

"Oh, so is that what you are going to do to me? Kill me next?"

His smile broadens as he chuckles. He really enjoyed watching me get worried about this revelation. It made him feel more powerful and in control."No, I would never kill you. Never. I may be a murderer, but I would never kill you, not in all the lives I will ever live would I kill you."

I smiled at this, it may have been twisted, but it was a sweet thing to say.

He had a huge wave of satisfaction flow through him as he saw me smiling at his words."You think that's sweet, do you? Do you actually believe the things I'm saying right now? Do you truly think I would never hurt you? Because if you do, I'm going to like playing with this even more than I have so far. Because I have some pretty sweet things I want to tell you."

"Today is your last day to make me fall in love with you. So give me everything you got."

He chuckled. So today was the day he had to make this plan work. The plan he'd been working on since the beginning of their sessions."You've already started to fall for me though. The way you were jealous when I slept with her, the way you got angry when I talked about her. If these reactions are anything to go by, you're already well on your way to being in love with me. So, do you still want everything I've got? Because I do intend to use everything I've got to finally seduce you."

"Am I really falling for you? Like I said give me everything you got."

He smirked, it was fun seeing me this eager. He felt a bit of a rush knowing that this was going to work. He was finally going to succeed at making me fall for him completely. So he was finally going to be able to use this to his full advantage. He did enjoy the control over me. This wasn't about the nurse anymore, now everything was about me. As for what he had to give to me, this is what he was going to use to make me fall in love with him. Just me and him now.

"Before I do anything else, I do want to know. Even after finding out that I killed her, the fact that she was the one I was sleeping with that night you got jealous. You're completely fine with all of that? You're still willing to fall in love with a murderer?"

"Yes."

He was honestly surprised, I was even more messed up than he originally thought. Just the fact that I am willing to accept his flaws is very attractive to him. I don't care that he is a murderer, or that he killed the woman he was having an affair with, I just want to fall in love with him. It was very hot.He was just about ready for the next step of his plan now. He was going to be able to enjoy this a bit longer though. I still seem pretty interested in him.He then leans back in his chair, taking time to think. Then his smile starts to broaden again. An idea of his was finally starting to shape itself in his head."Oh, I'm really starting to like you, you're interesting. There is only one way I can really prove my feelings to you. But before I do that, maybe I should give some more reasons and proof that your actually starting to fall for me. Let's see, what else do you need to realize that you're now falling for me?"

"A bold action."

He smirked as he thought of his next step. He was going to have to do something bold in order to get this to work."Oh, I think I have something in mind that should definitely qualify as a 'bold action.' Would you be okay if I did something pretty insane to prove that I mean what I'm saying?"

"Yes, I would."

That was even more intriguing to him. I was truly intrigued to see what he could come up with for this next step. He was pretty sure this next step was going to be the one to seal the deal."Good, the act I am about to do is one that I'm sure will leave you stunned. It may even surprise you. Are you okay with that?"

"I'm waiting."

He chuckles as I wait. I looked like I was really enjoying this. As my anticipation grew with his delay, he realized that this step was going to hit even harder now than if he had done it sooner. The way I was getting all excited over this was truly enjoyable to watch.He then stands up from the chair and steps closer to me. This is the point when he is going to do that one 'bold action' that will prove to me that I must be falling in love with him at this point.In quick movements, he grabs my shoulders and pulls my body close to his. We're both so close now, that we could almost kiss. His face is right now at eye level with mine."This is it, this 'bold action' of mine that will prove you're falling for me."

He then leans in even closer so that our foreheads are touching. Our hearts beat too fast in our chests. His breath washes over me, and his body radiates with heat. My body feels light and I feel like I could faint at any moment. I don't know what this means for him trying to make me fall in love with him, but this is definitely an action that will be hard for me to forget. Once again he leans even closer to me. Our faces are almost touching. His facial expression then changes to a small smile, almost predatory-like. The way he smiles at me while our faces are inches apart is very enticing. Our eyes lock together and I can swear that I can see the passion and desire radiating from his eyes. His breathing grows a bit heavier and he keeps our bodies close. I want to push him away but at the same time, I am so stunned I can't even move. He's so close my breathing is slow and shallow. It feels like I can see everything on his face, his pores, every small detail. He leans in a kisses me. This kiss has been building up for a while now. The way I finally kiss him back feels so powerful. The passion and desire he's radiating off of him is exhilarating and it feels like time has stopped in this moment. He kisses me with a hunger that is almost like instinct. As he kisses me he pulls me closer to his body, wanting to get as close to me as possible. I can feel every muscle in his body. This feeling is exhilarating in so many ways.

He watches me blush in response. I see the fire in his eyes turn to satisfaction. He's enjoying the way I respond to the intimacy that's now happening between us. Our breaths become even shallower. He knows that this moment of passion between us is having a powerful effect and he is loving it. He wants to kiss again already.

I take a step back and just stare at him, smiling from ear to ear, I don't even care that this was against our policy, I was just...happy in that moment.

He stares back at me. His eyes searched for any small reaction. How I feel after this moment is his only goal right now.He then tells me "You look so precious right now."

# CHAPTER 14

It had been a couple of days since I saw Archer, he was put in solitary confinement, tomorrow was his last day, but I couldn't wait any longer to see him. I bribed one of the nurses to let me through and she did. "Archer?"

He was sleeping when I walked in, but my voice must have woke him up, or perhaps it was just my presence. Either way, he now sat up in his bed. He rubbed his eyes to get the drowsiness out of him. "Freya? Is that really you?"

I rushed over to hug him. "Yes, how have you been doing in here?"

He was shocked at the sudden affection I gave him, but he didn't want to push me away. It felt like it had been ages since the last time he felt my warmth and body so close to his. He wrapped his arms around me, trying to return the affection. "It feels like it has been weeks. I have been going crazy in here. I missed you."

"I've missed you too. I just couldn't wait one more day to see you."

My words were the exact ones that he wanted to hear. He pulls my body even closer to him."Is that so? I've been wishing you were here to comfort me in this room these past couple of days. It's just so lonely, and I just couldn't help but think of you every single moment."

I smiled at his words. "Have you been eating while in here? Sleeping well?"

He chuckles in response. I was acting exactly like the concerned doctor would. As much as he wanted something else from me, he still felt very happy with how I was acting towards him. His tone then became a bit more serious."I have been getting by, I guess. But I haven't really been taking care of myself like I should've. I have just been too lost in my thoughts while in here. Not really sleeping that well either to be honest."

"Well, I brought something for you." I pulled out some cake that I had wrapped in a napkin. "I know your birthday was yesterday, but better late than never right?"

He couldn't help but let a smile take over his face once again. It had been so long since he last received any type of gift from anyone and this was certainly the perfect surprise. All of his thoughts of not being taken care of instantly started to disappear because of my kindness. As he takes the napkin-wrapped cake from me, he hugs me for the second time this day.

"Thank you so much for this. It really means a lot to have someone take care of me for once. I really do appreciate this."

"Of course."

He held the cake in his hands, the smile on his face was still present as we looked at each other."I do feel better now that you're here. The fact that you came here to visit me makes me feel like I finally matter somehow to someone. Thank you."

"You do matter to me."

That was the last piece of confirmation that he needed. He believed my words completely and I could see the satisfaction that it brought him in the small smile he gave me. He was starting to realize how deeply he was getting attached to me, and he was starting to love that feeling.*He leans in closer and whispers in my ear."And you matter to me. More than anyone I've ever met."

"That's actually what I came here to talk to you about."

My words got his full attention and he looked at me with an inquisitive look. Whatever I come to talk to him about, it has to be good news."What is it?"

"I wanted to tell you that you were right. I did fall in love with you after a week."

That was the best thing he could have hoped for me to say."I know I was right. You fell in love with me even sooner than a week. And honestly, I fell in love with you too, very quickly. This whole thing between us has been like an emotional dream. My time in here would have been unbearable without you, and all of this just confirms how much you mean to me."He looks around, making sure no one was listening."I think you should know that you are also the only person that matters to me in the world right now."

I smiled. "I have to go now, but I will see you tomorrow for our sessions!"

As I was about to turn to leave he grabbed a hold of my wrist and held my face closer to his."Just one thing before you go. Can I ask you one last question?"

"Yes."

He stares into my eyes to create the perfect mood."Do you trust me?"

"Yes, why do you ask?"

He smiles once again, my trust in him was the perfect feeling that he felt was the cherry on top."Because I want to ask you something that I know might sound crazy.Just please think about it before answering it."

"Ask me."

He pauses a bit before he finally decides to ask it."Would you do anything for me? And I mean anything..."

"Of course. Why?"

He looks very pleased with my answer. This was a huge accomplishment for him."I know this sounds a bit extreme, but I need you to prove your loyalty. I need your complete and absolute trust that you will always be mine, and that you will always follow any order I give you. Would you still do it, even if you don't completely understand it?"

"Okay."

He chuckles a bit, realizing that I didn't even have any hesitation to my request. He could already tell I was completely attached to him by your responses. He just needed to test out my loyalty and I immediately agreed to it."Good. I'll be giving you your first order soon."

# Chapter 15

T he whole night I thought of Archer, I wondered what my first order was going to be. I got ready for work and headed out the door. I was stopped by a note left on my doorstep. "You threw away my chocolate?" Was all that it said. I am bewildered by who could be leaving these notes on my door. I walked to my car to see a brick had been thrown through my window. I was shocked. I did not hear anything throughout the night.

I decided to call a cab because I did not want to drive with a broken window, it was far too cold for that. I arrived at the hospital and hurried inside my boss' office, but he was not there. I wondered if he took off for the family business that was so personal.

I went to my office to see my favorite murderer sitting in his usual seat waiting for our sessions to begin. He was waiting very patiently, and he could tell that something was definitely on my mind. My face said it all. I was deep in thought and he couldn't wait to find out what caused that expression. He was going to push me, to be honest and tell him what was on my mind.

"You got that look on your face where you are thinking of something but can't decide if you should say it or not. What is it?"

I sat in my seat and stared at him for a moment, I was curious. "You said you were going to give an order soon? What is it?" I asked.

My reaction caught him off guard. I was quicker to ask him about the order than he thought. Just how eager I seemed to get an order from him just showed him how much he had me wrapped around his finger. I was ready. A smile spreads across his face as he waits a moment more before finally giving me the order. "I need... I order you to be my nurse. The only nurse that ever treats me. It's time for me to test the limits of your loyalty."

I was stunned, I'm not sure how I could manage to pull this off, but I wanted to show my loyalty. My boss was gone for the day so I couldn't put in the request today, so I will put in the request tomorrow. "Okay, I will become your nurse. I will also still be your shrink."

This was the perfect opportunity for him to push me further. My eagerness to show my loyalty is making it easy for him to manipulate me. I was so quick to agree to be his nurse that he couldn't help but try to push it even more. "Good, but I would like you to make me your only patient as well. I don't want someone else getting the attention that you could be giving me."

I nod my head, "Understood."

I didn't care how vulnerable I was making myself to his tactics, I genuinely felt like he loved me and maybe I was dumb for that. But I was okay with it, I felt happy.

My quick response to that statement also made him feel very satisfied. I didn't argue at all or hesitate. This was going as flawless as possible."Good. And just one more thing..."

"Yes?"

He can't help but smile, seeing my eagerness. He needed to see how far he could take this. I was doing everything that he had asked so far with no hesitation and no arguments which was very pleasing to him."I'm sure that by now you understand how attached I am getting to you. Would you be willing to do anything for me? Even if it means abandoning your career?

I was shocked, I had busted my ass for this career and he wants me to throw it away? I know he said no questions ask but I just couldn't help myself. "May I ask why? Like how would me abandoning my career benefit you?"

He chuckled and it felt like he enjoyed my response. I had the guts to ask questions even after he said no questions asked. My attitude really was getting him hooked."I need you all to myself. I think I have earned that right by now. How can you truly be loyal to me if your other patients get in the way of the time that we spend together? How can you truly be loyal if you aren't completely devoted to me?"

"I will cut off all my patients as we agreed. However, my career gives me access to be your nurse and be your shrink so I can see you every day. Are you asking me to abandon my career in the future IF you are ever let out of this place?"

He was very impressed with how I was thinking ahead. I was looking at the long-term picture which was very convenient for him. "That is exactly what I want. You are right that you need this career right now so that you can have access to me on a daily basis, and I need that. But once I am released from here then I want you to quit your career and abandon it all just for me."

I paused for a moment. "But, what if you don't ever get out?"

My concern made him feel so powerful in such a strange way. I was worried as if what he was asking wasn't a given of course. He had so much faith in me and it was making me feel very special. "Don't ever think that way. I will get out of here eventually. It's not a matter of IF, I will get out of here. The day that happens I would like that you quit your career and abandon everything to be with me, like I said. Is that clear?"

"Understood."

My continued responses are putting him in a very good mood. I was so obedient and submissive to him. It was making all his desires come to life. My loyalty is truly unmatched. I was getting lost in his eyes, wondering what the future would hold for us when my phone rang. It was an unknown number.

"Hello?" I asked.

"Hello. The is detective Gardner with the police department. Would you mind coming down to the police station?"

My heart dropped. "May I ask what this is about?"

"Ma'am, someone broke into your house."

"Of course, I am leaving work now." I gathered my things and gave a brief overview of what had just happened and ran out the door. I called a cab and they picked me up and drove me to the police station. I ran into the station and they had me sit in the Chief's office. He walked into his office and sat down with a warm smile.

"Hello, how are you?"

"I'm worried, what happened to my house?"

"I have one question for you before we continue. This man was caught breaking into your house. Do you know this man?" He sits down a picture on the table and slides it over to me.

I picked it up and my eyes widened. "That's my boss."

# Chapter 16

The officer got quiet for a moment, he was thinking of his next words to say. "Do you know why your boss would want to break into your house?"

I didn't know, I was surprised. "No, I don't."

"Well, we questioned for a few moments. I don't think he was there to rob you, I think he was there FOR you."

My jaw slightly dropped and my heart sank. "What makes you say that? Is that what he told you?"

He cleared his throat. "No, but he didn't take anything from your house, he was just creeping inside. Your house was not turned upside down, it was neat, aside from the broken window. We did ask his intentions and he just refused to answer. We are cops, it's our job to put two and two together."

I was stunned, I was shocked. Why would he do this? "May I speak to him?"

The officer raised his eyebrow and nodded. "If that's what you wished."

I stood up and he directed me to the interrogation room. When I walked into the room, he looked surprised. I was so angry I could slap him. "You have got to believe me. They got the wrong man." He stated.

I stared at him, I didn't believe him. "Why were you not at work today?"

He was silent for a few seconds. "I was at work."

"I went to your office, everyone said you were out."

"Oh, why did you go into my office?" He smirked.

I was disgusted. I rolled my eyes. "For work business. Why else?"

He leaned on the table and looked into my eyes. "You know we have some sort of chemistry. You can't deny it."

I recoiled. "We have no chemistry! I find you annoying."

He was so cocky. "Then why go on those coffee dates?"

I rolled my eyes. "Because I felt bad for you, that's why."

He seemed angry at this response. "Oh? Don't tell me you are falling for Archer. Is that why you have been so difficult to get to? I will have you fired and I will have him killed if that's the case."

"Why are you being so cruel?" I was absolutely horrified.

He chuckled. "Because, I always get my way, and he is currently standing in the way of that."

I was outraged by this, I stood up and walked out of the room. I was pissed. I wanted him locked up. I told the officers I wanted to press every charge I could. Before I left, I went back to the interrogation room one last time. "Were you the one leaving those creepy presents at my door?"

He smirked. "Creepy? Is that what you call it?"

I scoffed. "Yes, creepy. You knew I wasn't interested in you in a romantic way, and yet you left CREEPY presents and notes along with it."

He rolled his eyes. "You are just ungrateful, what if I had left you a brand new car at your doorstep? I bet it wouldn't have been a creepy present then."

"I wouldn't have accepted even then." I spat out. I stormed out of the interrogation room and as I was leaving he yelled.

"I will get rid of him, you know."

I stopped dead in my tracks and turned to look at him. I shot daggers at him, I was not going to waste any more words with this man. I left and went home. I was upset, I cried the whole car ride home. Would he really get rid of him? I am sure he was going to get locked up, especially after basically just admitting murder in front of the officers. I was exhausted and I just wanted a nap.

When I arrived home, I walked straight to my room and crashed. I woke up a couple of hours later to my phone going off. I was getting text messages from my boss. I was confused considering he should be locked up, how and why was he texting me?

"Im free." His first message stated.

"Funny how having a huge salary can make things change very quickly." That was the next message.

He had paid his bond and I am sure he even bribed with his money. How sick these cops were. They were acting so concerned and then let him go all in a couple of hours. How disgusting. I was sure to be fired the next day, I was anxious because now I had no job, and I'm sure writing a letter of recommendation was out of the question. Was he really going to kill Archer next? I was dreading tomorrow. I needed to speak with Archer before things got too out of hand.

I woke up the next day feeling defeated, before I headed into my office, a nurse came and told me Johnathan needed to see me. I dragged my feet to his office and sat in the chair across from him waiting to see what he had to say.

"Well, good morning to you too." He said in a cocky tone with a smirk.

I rolled my eyes. "I assumed you are going to fire me now?" I said nonchalantly. On the inside, I was terrified, because that would mean that I would have to leave now, and I need to speak to Archer.

He laughed at this. "No, I am not going to fire you."

My eyes widened. Just the other day he said he would and now he is saying he's not, I'm sure he had a plan as to why he is not going to fire me yet.

"You said you were the other day. What changed your mind."

He cleared his throat. "At some point, Archer will have to die. You being his shrink and all, you are going to have to watch and participate in his death. That gives me much more satisfaction than just firing you."

My breath caught in my chest. I was furious at how cruel this man could be. I got up and walked to my office where I saw Archer sitting in my office. I slammed my notebooks on my desk and before he could get any words out I stated, "We are going to have to kill Johnathan."

# Chapter 17

He almost choked at my sudden request. Did I really just say what he thought I did? His heart started beating rapidly at the idea. No way I was actually going to help me kill someone. Of course, he played it all cool on the outside though."So, why is it that we need to kill Johnathan?"

"Because he is going to try and kill you. He was the mystery man I was seeing. he started to leave creepy presents at my house and while I was at work yesterday he broke into my house to do, I don't know what. However, I can get an idea. He told me just moments ago that he wanted to kill you because he knew I was in love with you."

I gave a damn good reason to kill him. Knowing that he broke into my house and knowing how obsessive he was, he had a good idea about what he wanted to do."And you seriously wanted to kill him for that? I mean I'm really flattered that you would go through all that trouble for me and I can definitely see that you love me, but why not just use the police?"

"Because the police arrested him for breaking into my house, then he gave them money to bribe himself out. They have proven not to be so helpful."

This just keeps getting more and more interesting. If the police can be bought by him then that is very suspicious and really does warrant him being taken care of. He could do something about it himself but it was my idea to kill him so he let me take the charge."Alright well then how do we plan on doing it? I trust you to plan the whole thing."

Well, no. I sorted just told you what I wanted and hoped you had an idea. You are kind of a murderer. Isn't this your thing?"

I was really not going to back down from ordering him around. He had to admit, I definitely made my point. In terms of this type of situation, this was his area of expertise. He couldn't help but be impressed by my forwardness once again."Alright, give me a few minutes to think. I'll come up with a plan for us."

A few minutes of silence went by. I was anxiously waiting for his response. "Well?"

My anxiousness just gave him another feeling of power and he couldn't help but enjoy it. Once again I was letting him take control of the situation and that was very satisfying in his eyes. He was still thinking but he didn't wanna make me wait too long for his answer so he decided to just spit out the plan that he was forming."I think I know how to kill him. We gotta get him alone where no one can see us and then I'll make sure to take care of him. Simple as that. I can do it easily."

After a few more minutes of discussing the plan, we agreed to get Johnathan alone before Archer strangles him to death. We can't risk getting any sedatives or tools because it could cause others to suspect us. We decided to go forward with the plan tonight.Johnathan had a conference call late tonight which would mean the building would be empty and it gave us a perfect opportunity to kill him. We agreed I would stay in my office as he went to handle the business then he would rush into my office afterward.

He nodded his head, he was satisfied with the plan.We both knew that this was exactly what we needed to do. It was a perfect plan, and he was going to see this through. He was starting to see a potential future with me."Then that's what we'll do. I look forward to handling him tonight. I'll take care of him without causing any suspicion on either you or me."

"Great! Before you go, I will cut off the security cameras in the hallway outside his office so there will be no proof of you being there."

That was perfect and a very smart way to cover our tracks. "Clever as always. I really don't see how this plan can fail if we follow all these steps that we discussed. I'll be going now, to make sure that this entire plan is absolutely executed flawlessly."

He returned to his room while we waited for the hours to go by. Hour after hour, nurse after nurse slowly started to descend from the building. I was getting more anxious as the time grew closer. The security guard went on break for the next 2 hours. After he left I snuck my way into the security office and cut off the camera leading into the hallway. Everything seemed to be going smoothly and the plan was ready. I went to one of the doctors who was guarding Archer's room and told them we had another session for the night and he let him out, we walked right back to my office to go over the final details before the plan was executed.

The whole plan was set to go perfectly right. With the cameras down and the guards on break, all the cards are in our favor for this plan to go smoothly. He was already getting a few butterflies in his stomach as we walked into my office for this final conversation before he did what he was going to do.

Archer left and I waited patiently for his return. He waited down the hall from Johnathan's office. After a few minutes, Johnathan walked out. He locked his office and headed down the hall. Archer slowly walked in front of him. They were a couple of feet apart from each other.

"Hello, Johnthan," Archer said with a sister tone and smile.

Johnathan was feeling slightly uncomfortable realizing that he was alone with Archer. "Why are you out of your room?" he asked trying to appear calm and dominate.

Archer chuckled and looked at him for a few uncomfortable minutes. "I'm here to do something I have been aching to do for a while."

# Chapter 18

Johnathan was stunned. "What do you mean?"

Archer smirked. He didn't even reply. He lunged on top of him and started to choke. Johnathan didn't even seem to want to fight back, he struggled a bit but just gave up in the end. He stood up and looked at what seemed to be a dead man. "Pity. I wanted a bigger fight."

He had a smug look on his face. He stepped into my office with his hands in his pockets, waiting for me to say whatever comment I wanted to make. He was smiling a bit, knowing I wanted to say something about him being so quick to take him out.

I was shocked. It didn't take him long. I stared at him. "Is it done?...."

"Yes. The guy was a complete disgrace. Not only did he have the audacity to break into your house, but he also said he was going to kill me in front of everyone. Just because he couldn't handle the fact that I am so much more appealing to you than he could ever hope to be. It was insulting that someone like him thought he was even close to my level."

I laughed at his strange remark. I ran up to him and kissed him, all this adrenaline made me excited and felt powerful.

This sudden kiss was unexpected but not unwelcome. The rush he felt from being able to kill this bastard and the fact I was so happy over it just fueled his attraction to me even more. I stepped back from kissing him and took a deep breath. "So what now?"

He smirked and was just enjoying these sudden bursts of excitement. He couldn't help but admire how we just completed this task together. I feel like we made some kind of unspoken bond."Now," He got closer to me, making sure to be right in my personal space, "I think it's time we celebrate."

My face turned red. I trailed my fingers on his shirt and smirked. "How do you suggest we do that?"

He smiled even more at the fact that my face did indeed turn red. I was definitely embarrassed about the situation and my sudden attraction to him was very clear. He couldn't help but feel pleased at how this whole situation has been playing out."I'm not one to beat around the bush. You know what I want."

I smiled big and kissed him. I wanted more than ever, I wanted to feel his skin, I wanted to breathe him in, I wanted all of him. He picked me up and threw me on the desk. He wrapped his arm around me to deepen our kiss. I tugged at his shirt indicating that I wanted it off. He understood and took it off as I also took mine off. He smirked at the sight of my shirtless. He came back for another kiss as he pushed my skirt up and rubbed my thighs. I wrapped my legs around his waist. His body felt perfect against mine, I wanted more. I wanted all of him. I removed my underwear and he came right back in between my legs kissing me.

All thoughts have disappeared. Him sleeping with the nurse then killing her, him killing my boss, all of it was gone. I wanted to enjoy my moment with him. He groaned as he used his hand to feel how wet I was. I gasped at his touch, his hands were cold and it felt amazing. He took a step back and glanced at me.

"You look so damn perfect right now." He removed his pants. He smiled as he pulled down his boxers slightly revealing how erect he was. My eyes grew with excitement, I wanted it all. My eyes begged for him, and he saw that. He loved it. He chuckled before returning to me. He grabbed my hips and pulled me closer to him. Right as he was about to make his entrance, My office door busted open. It was Johnathan.

My eyes grew with fear. I looked at Archer, I thought he was dead. I couldn't believe it. Why was he here? He had two security guards with him. He pointed at Archer as he gasped for air.

"Him. Get him." With that, the guards grabbed him and his clothes and hauled him away. After Archer had left, Johnathan stepped towards to me with this menacing look. "You just made killing him so easy." He left my office. I sat there, half-naked, and tears in my eyes. I couldn't believe it. Archer was as good as dead because of me.

# Chapter 19

The next day had come and I was dreading walking into work. I did not want to go, but I did. I made my way into the building and headed straight to go see Archer. The doctors stopped me so I couldn't continue any further. "Johnathan had ordered us not to let you through."

My heart was aching and you could see it on my face. "Please. Just give me 5 minutes."

The doctor was hesitant but he could see the hurt in my eyes. "5 minutes. Thats all. Then you must go." I thanked him and ran into the room. I saw Archer strapped in his chair and he gave me a cold look.

As soon as he saw me walk in, he got a sudden surge of anger. He thought he was supposed to be the smart one here, but he was too idiotic to realize I wouldn't betray him.He immediately yelled out, "You think you could me up? Are you crazy?"

I was stunned. I didn't set him up, how could he think that? "I...I would never."

He scoffed. "You came up with this plan to kill him, then I get caught. Did you want me dead? Was that your plan all along?"

I stared at him in disbelief. "No! I love you, Archer. I wouldn't."

He just stared at me with this cold glare. "I never loved you. I was just using you. I needed you in my plan to escape this hellhole and you seemed to fall for it."

My eyes filled with tears. He... He didn't love me? "You don't love me? It was all a lie?"

He smirked at seeing my heart breaking in my eyes. He just nodded and stopped talking.

"Archer you have to believe me, I would never do this." I pleaded.

He just stared at the wall in front of him, not even glancing at me. He was like the Archer I met on my first day here.

I was about to speak but there was a knock at the door. It was the doctor letting me know that my 5 minutes was up. I sighed in defeat and headed towards the door, before I left I stopped and mumbled. "....I love you." And then I left.

I went back to my office in tears and saw Johnathan waiting for me there. He had this smug look on his face. He loved seeing me hurt like this. He was filled with joy. "Your little boyfriend will be gone soon, don't worry." He chuckled.

I was disgusted with him. I wished I had just committed the act myself. I wanted him gone. I walked up to him and slapped him. He just laughed in my face. "It is worth it. I'll let you slap me around, in the end, your pain and suffering will be worth it."

His smug look made me want to slap him 10 times harder. Before he left he turned to look at me, "Once I get the motion approved. I will personally come and let you know when his death date is." He laughed before walking off.

My heart sank. His death date. I couldn't believe it. I knew he would want him gone, but I didn't think he would make a public spectacle of his death. He was mocking him. Determination filled me. I needed to fix this, I needed to stop it, but I didn't know how.

Hours had gone by and I was at my desk just filing paperwork, they needed all this information on Archer before they could proceed with his death. I was taking my time to try and prolong it. As I was deep into my work a knock was placed on my door. It was Johnathan. I internally rolled my eyes before looking up at him.

"I just wanted to come by and let you know that tonight will be the night."

My breath was caught in my chest. "Why so soon? I haven't finished the paperwork."

He laughed. "Well, considering he murdered a nurse and tried to kill me within a month, they see his behavior deteriorating. So it was decided for tonight. They can get the paperwork from you after he is dead."

My face saddened. "How will he die?" I asked, not really wanting to know the answer.

"Lethal Injection. Performed by you." He smiled.

My eyes grew wide with shock. I shook my head. "No. I can't."

He seemed amused by my rejection. "Ah, but you have to. You were deemed by the board to kill him. It would be illegal if you went against their wishes."

I felt defeated. I had to. He left the room and I just cried. I couldn't bring myself to do this. I was ordered to go to the room with the sedatives. I was examining all of the vials. My heart was broken the more time went by. The doctor handed me the lethal injection and I was ordered to bring it to the room where the death would be happening.

The room was empty, knowing that in a couple of hours, it would be full of an audience and a dying Archer. I couldn't bring myself to imagine it. Imagine him looking at me as he took his final breath. I started crying at just the thought of it. There was a doctor in the room with me, he placed a hand on my shoulder. "It will be over soon."

My heart saddened. He could see the pain in my eyes, he knew this was going to hurt and he felt compassion for me. He walked away to finish sterilizing the room and setting up for tonight's events. I walked back to my office with a heavy heart, I just wanted to see him one last time, but I couldn't. It would be too risky.

Hours had gone by and I only had one hour left before I had to perform. I was racking my brain with ideas, trying to come up with a plan to save him, but nothing seemed to come to mind. I felt so drained and defeated. I wanted to run away, I wanted to cry. Then I became angry. He never loved me? That thought kept repeating itself.

All the affection, all the kind words, everything... It wasn't real? Maybe he deserved to die then. He manipulated me so well I actually believed he loved me and cared for me. I was getting beyond upset, I was getting more and more upset as the time grew closer. I stormed into Johnathan's office and plopped myself into his chair.

He looked at me in confusion. "Come to change my mind?" He asked me in an amused tone.

"No," I stated.

His face grew puzzled. "Just hours ago you were hurt, and now you don;t want to do anything to try and fix this?"

I looked at the clock to see I had 10 minutes left before it was time. A smile grew on my face. "Im ready."

# Epilogue

The time had come, it was time for Archer to die. That manipulative shit. My heart was hurting but for a different reason, it hurt because I was lied to. I made my way to the bathroom to get dressed in the clothes I was given to wear for this event. I put on the white coat and the protective scrub to wear on top. I walked outside to meet up with the other nurses and doctors. We were all wearing our assigned protective clothes and walked down the long hallway.

The hallway felt longer than usual, but eventually, we did arrive at the door. I was last to come inside. Archer was not there yet, they had sent a couple of doctors to go grab him and strap him down in a wheelchair. A few minutes had gone by and he was wheeled in. I looked out into the room, I couldn't see them, but I knew they could see me. There was a news reporter and a couple of my coworkers, I knew that much. Johnathan came in to make his personal appearance, he wanted to make a speech.

"I am sad to say that we will be losing one of our patients today, but nothing seemed to be helping him progress." Even though he acted sad, I knew deep down he was jumping with joy. "Today his death will be assisted by Freya Jones, Justin Moore, and Amelia Perkins. These wonderful nurses and doctor have done their best to assist Archer Williams in his time here, they have grown to care for him and were deeply disturbed by his recent actions. We thought it would be best for him to have the people he dealt with on a daily basis to be the last thing he sees before going on his way after death."

He concluded his speech with a sad sigh, but I knew it was fake. All of it was fake. He didn't feel a drop of sadness, a drop of remorse, nothing. "We will begin the death shortly, however, I feel like each of the nurses and doctor should give their own speech for Archer."

Justin was first in line. "Archer was one of my most difficult patients. He fought for every feeding, and he screamed during every medication time. However, I would like to believe that somewhere deep down inside of him, he was sane and knew how to love. I liked to believe that he knew how to care. It saddens me to see one of my patients go, but I believe God has plans for him."

Everyone clapped after his speech and next was Amelia. "I would like to believe that Mr. Willams had a precious understanding of human life. I don't want to believe that he is dying a heartless man. He was difficult, but I like to believe it was just a front." She kept her speech short and sweet and then next was me.

I didn't prepare a speech, so I went on a whim. "I'm not really sure what to say, so I guess I will say what's on my heart. When I first met Archer, I was intrigued by him. He didn't seem like just any ordinary killer, he seemed human. As our sessions continued, I got to learn a lot about him. He was caring, he was human, and he had feelings. He was given a shit life, and I felt for him. A few sessions later he admitted that he wanted me to fall in love with him. I didn't believe that I could ever fall in love with a killer...but I did. As much as I hate to admit it, I did. I fell in love with him completely. He kissed me, showed me affection, and treated me with kindness. Later I found out it was all a lie. He admitted it was a lie. Deep down, I don't believe that, but I could just be manipulating myself to believe my own lie." I glanced at Archer and he was looking straight ahead. My words didn't seem to affect him.

It was time to start the killing. They prepared him. They moved him to the chair and strapped him down, I could see the panic start to settle in him, but he wasn't going to show it. Amelia and Justin stepped aside and let me gather the tools I needed. There was a syringe on the table and gloves and a sanitization wipe.

I grabbed my gloves and put them on, I grabbed the wipe and wiped his skin. I then reached for the syringe and pulled it out of my pocket. I stared at him in the eyes and he looked angry. He felt betrayed and I knew that. I smiled at him before I stuck the needle in his arm. I slowly pushed the liquid into his skin and everyone watched him as his eyes fluttered back. His eyes were finally closed and his head fell down. The room was filled with silence. He was gone.

I stared at Johnathan and smiled then I released the straps that were binding him. The doctor started to clean up the table with all the tools on it and spoke.

"The syringe is still on the table. She didn't use the lethal injection!"

Johnathan stormed to me pinned me against the wall and screamed. "WHAT DID YOU DO?"

Moments after he spoke, Archer's eyes opened and he stood up.